A
HARLEQUIN
Book

ABOVE RUBIES

by

MARY CUMMINS

HARLEQUIN BOOKS

Winnipeg • Canada   New York • New York

ABOVE RUBIES

First published in 1969 by Mills & Boon Limited,
50 Grafton Way, Fitzroy Square, London, England.

Harlequin Canadian edition published November, 1969
Harlequin U.S. edition published February, 1970

Standard Book Number: 373-51350-X.

Printed in Canada

CHAPTER 1

MERRY came downstairs, quietly, a small suit-case in her hand, the rest of her luggage piled in the hall. The taxi was due in another fifteen minutes, just enough time to say goodbye to Aunt Elizabeth and Uncle George.

They were both sitting in the lounge, and as she walked in Merry could feel the strength of their disapproval in the atmosphere. It was a large room, ostentatious rather than tasteful. Everything had been chosen with a view to the maximum of ease and comfort, but on Merry it had had the opposite effect, and in the three years she had lived in Carlisle, she had come to feel that it was ready to smother her. Now she could hardly believe that in a few more minutes she would be leaving it all behind, and it was difficult to keep the elation out of her voice.

"I'm ready now, Aunt Elizabeth. Everything's packed, and I've left the room tidy. I do hope you'll both come and visit me after I've settled down at Kilbraggan."

Elizabeth Neilson ignored her for a full minute, carefully leafing over her glossy maga-zine pages with long slender white fingers, then looked up at her niece.

5

"We can only hope you won't regret your decision, Merry," she said coolly. "Beau Ness hardly seems a suitable house for a young girl of nineteen to live in by herself. I don't know what Ellen was thinking of to leave it all to you. After all, she was as much my friend as your mother's, and Sylvia has as much claim as you have . . ."

"She thought I would love it, Aunt Elizabeth, and I do."

". . . and it seems to be singularly puzzling that she should only think of you," went on her aunt, as though Merry hadn't spoken, while Uncle George cleared his throat and rustled his paper. "You must have influenced her in some way, Merry, when you went to stay with her on holidays, instead of travelling on the Continent like dear Sylvia. A girl should broaden her horizons and not insinuate herself with a maiden lady."

"Oh, but I didn't . . ."

"Though who would have thought that Ellen Blayne had a bad heart? She was only in her fifties, after all. It should be a warning to you, Merry, not to live in that house alone. You should have taken your Uncle George's advice, and let him sell it for you, and invest the money. Shouldn't she, George?"

"Very unwise of you, my dear," her uncle rumbled, clearing his throat again. "Might be difficult to sell in a few months' time. Mortgages

6

are hard these days, and it's getting to the wrong time of year for Kilbraggan. These Scotch villages . . ."

"Scottish," mumbled Merry.

". . . are all very well in the height of the season, but they're hopeless in winter. No good at all. It might take overspill from Hillington, but it isn't a very smart area."

Merry glanced at the clock, wishing the taxi would come soon. She'd been over all this before with both Aunt Elizabeth and Uncle George, while her cousin, Sylvia, sulked disdainfully. Her Aunt Ellen had predicted trouble for her when she asked her to promise to look after Beau Ness.

"They'd just sell my lovely house, darling," she had said, looking round the beautiful long sitting-room with the old polished furniture and brasses which winked in the firelight. "They'd never love Beau Ness as we do. They couldn't even love *you*, though your father was Elizabeth's only brother. I wanted to take you when he died in that plane crash on his way home from Nigeria. That was when you were at that awful boarding school."

"It wasn't so bad," said Merry, smiling with affection at the one woman who had really loved her since her mother died. "As you should know!"

"It was in your mother's day, and mine."

"Times have changed, though, Aunt Ellen,

7

and Daddy had to leave me somewhere. He didn't earn much as a missionary."

"Well, you won't earn much as a writer," said Ellen, "but if it's what you want to do, then stick to it like glue. Don't let Elizabeth push you into anything."

"I won't," promised Merry.

It hadn't been easy, though, and Merry had already spent three months in the office, typing for Uncle George, when the sad news came that Aunt Ellen had died and bequeathed her Beau Ness, together with a small income.

Aunt Elizabeth had been furious, as she considered it a great mistake for Merry to have property of her own. The fact that Sylvia had twice inherited legacies made no difference, in her opinion. Besides, now that she was losing Merry, she was loth to admit that she would miss her, having found her willing and useful. Even George would find her difficult to replace, and would have to pay a trained girl a ridiculous salary for doing the same work.

"I suppose Sylvia is out with Graham," said Merry, hoping to change the subject, and wishing fervently that the hands of the clock would move.

"Not an ideal choice of young man," disapproved Aunt Elizabeth, "but dear Sylvia is so popular. I expect she feels sorry for him, though she's much too beautiful to throw herself away on a mere schoolteacher."

Merry felt a pang of sympathy for the earnest bespectacled young man who had once been her own boy-friend. He had so obviously fallen under the spell of her lovely cousin. Sylvia's spun-gold hair fell round a pretty, piquant face with unusual slanting eyes. Her looks suggested a hidden depth and intelligence which Merry knew were both lacking. She'd never been close friends with her cousin, who had treated her like a poor relation and who had sulked ever since Beau Ness became hers.

"Here's the taxi now," she cried, jumping up as wheels crunched in the drive. "Goodbye, Aunt Elizabeth . . . Uncle George." She bent to kiss their unresponsive faces. "Thank you for looking after me over the past three years. I . . . I've appreciated having a home."

The silence indicated that she had a queer way of showing her appreciation.

"Come and see me, won't you?" she repeated.

"Sylvia will probably want to come, but we prefer not to travel during cold weather," said her aunt. "Goodbye, Merry. I hope you won't regret this."

"Goodbye, my dear," nodded Uncle George.

Merry ran down the steps of Fairlawn, the modern, expensive house which had sheltered her for those three years, and which had never seemed a real home in spite of all the luxurious thick carpeting and the most expensive and prettiest of furnishings. Beau Ness would be almost primitive by comparison, but already her heart was lifting as the taxi swung round at the gate, and into the main road. The journey ahead would take a good eight hours, and it would be early evening by the time she reached Kilbraggan, but Mrs. Cameron, the housekeeper, had promised to stay on and would have a warm fire and supper ready for her. Merry had known Mrs. Cameron ever since she was a schoolgirl.

"It will be a real pleasure, Miss Merry," she wrote. "I was feared you'd be selling the house and we'd have another stranger among us. Rossie House has been empty since old Mr. Ross-Findlater died, and now there's business folk living in it—the Kilpatricks from Hillington. Mr. Benjamin's at the Cot House, too. I doubt if you know him, but he's a funny one . . ."

Merry smiled as she sat in the Scottish train which would carry her straight to Glasgow before she had to change into a local train. She wondered what the Kilpatricks would be like, and Mr. Benjamin, the funny one, that being Mrs. Cameron's favourite expression to cover anything that was odd. She spent the rest of the journey weaving delightful stories round his no-doubt strange appearance, and she hadn't tired of the game when Joe Weir's taxi finally deposited her at the door of Beau Ness.

"Mercy on us, Miss Merry," cried Mrs. Cameron, hurrying to help carry her luggage into the house. "You'll be weary to death of your journey. I've a pot of broth ready and you can sup a wee bit before you go to bed. I've put a piggy in the bed, though it's been kept well aired since . . . Oh, well, we'll not be talking of that now."

Merry nodded, too tired to say very much beyond the first greetings. She'd sup her broth because she knew she'd never be allowed into bed without it, but after that she'd be glad to crawl between the freshest of white sheets which always smelled of lavender.

It was wonderful to have Mrs. Cameron to fuss over her, and tuck her up in bed. She was hardly conscious of her leaving the room.

The following morning Merry awoke with a curious feeling of well-being. In one sense Kilbraggan was so quiet, but not in another, for the birds were singing joyfully, and not so far away she could hear the cows lowing in a field.

Merry lay quietly allowing the curious mixture of reality and strangeness to soak into her mind. This was Aunt Ellen's bedroom, the biggest and most comfortable in Beau Ness, but Mrs. Cameron had been wise enough to move small knicknacks she'd always loved, from the bedroom which had been hers. Now she lay looking at a favourite picture of a Highland loch, and reached out to fondle her china Scottie which now sat on the table beside her bed.

Merry lay remembering the long, carefree

holidays she'd spent in Beau Ness when she and Aunt Ellen had roamed the neighbourhood together, coming in ravenous to eat Mrs. Cameron's nourishing foods which were planned to put some beef on to Miss Merry. For a short time she allowed a few tears to trickle down her cheeks for the absence of Ellen Blayne, who had been her mother's very dearest friend, though it was not a complete absence. It seemed as though the spirit of the older woman still lurked in quiet corners, watchful of the fact that her beloved house was still cared for, and loved, its warmth still being used as a real home.

"That's what it is," said Merry aloud. "A real home."

The first home she'd had since she was twelve, she thought happily, and in a mood of exultation she slipped back the warm blankets and stood on the thick sheepskin rug by the window, gently pulling back the curtains. No one could call it a "braw" day, but although grey, the sky was calm without lowering black clouds scudding across. Merry had seen Kilbraggan in all its moods, and knew that this was "no sich a bad day"—good enough, in fact, for her to go for a brisk walk. Soon she would have to get down to serious writing again, but she was pleased to give herself a few days to settle in, and decided to fix the following Monday as her first working day.

Merry had had very little success so far,

though she knew that only to the few does success come easily. She'd sold a few articles and one short story. Now she would like to try a full-length novel with, perhaps, a few more articles and short stories to send out, for more immediate results.

Aunt Elizabeth had disapproved of her writing, accusing her of wasting her time on rubbish, but Ellen had always encouraged her, putting on her large reading glasses to inspect her latest manuscript, and criticising it intelligently.

"This one doesn't quite come off, does it, Merry?" she would ask, handing back a short story. "One of your characters . . . Joe Bell . . . has behaved rather out of character, if you know what I mean. He would never suddenly go to the funfair, after avoiding such a thing all his life. You'll have to give him a reason for going."

Merry had choked down her defence of the story, and had later admitted that Aunt Ellen was right.

"You've got a talent for making characters come to life, though," the older woman continued. "We mustn't waste that. I think you ought to spend some time on your writing while you're here."

Merry had done her best work while sitting at Aunt Ellen's big desk in her small study. Now she hoped to work there more permanently. Her income would be sufficient to feed her, and pay the household bills, including Mrs. Cameron's wages, but she would have to earn her own pocket money, and even some of her clothing allowance, and she loved clothes.

Though her wardrobe was fairly small, she had always bought wisely, and had often turned out to parties looking every bit as elegant as Sylvia. In fact, many people considered Merry's dark chestnut-brown hair, contrasting with vivid blue eyes and a peaches-and-cream complexion, even more lovely than Sylvia's fair beauty, and Aunt Elizabeth had often been infuriated over hearing comparisons made in Merry's favour.

She would have no cause for jealousy at the moment, thought Merry, as she slid her long legs into olive green slacks and slipped on a pale primrose jersey. Strong walking brogues and a brown suede jacket completed her outfit, and she slipped quietly downstairs for a short walk before breakfast.

"You're never going out at this time, Miss Merry," cried Mrs. Cameron, scandalised. "After a day like you had yesterday! You'll have yourself worn away to a wee shadow. You'll need some good porridge to stick to your ribs first."

"I was only going a short way, to work up an appetite," explained Merry.

"Oh, aye. You've gone a 'short way' before and we've had to come seeking you for your dinner. Now come on, Miss Merry, and eat up a good breakfast, there's a good lass."

Merry sighed. She had often heard Aunt Ellen being lectured just like this, and had caught the twinkle in her eye. Now the mantle had fallen on her, yet there was a quiet and relaxed feeling of well-being in having Mrs. Cameron look after her. She began to appreciate how Aunt Ellen had felt. It was so nice to be cherished by someone.

"I thocht you'd want to see the house, too," said Mrs. Cameron, "now that it's yours."

"We'll leave that till later." This time Merry's tone was decided. "I'll get some fresh air first."

It was after ten by the time Merry felt energetic enough to go for a walk through the village. Kilbraggan was a tiny place with two rows of small whitewashed cottages interspersed with wee shops which sold most commodities for daily needs. Houses straggled on the outskirts, standing in their own grounds behind trees and hedges.

Beau Ness was fairly small, with only six rooms, but it had been substantially built and its patina was delightful. Merry stuck her hands into the pockets of her jacket, and felt the pride of ownership surge through her as she looked back at its ivy-covered walls and twinkling latticed windows.

A few yards up the road she could see the

cottage which housed the "funny one", now known to Merry as Benjamin Brendan, commercial artist, and behind the trees she could see the tall chimneys of Rossie House which had belonged to the Ross-Findlaters for so many years, but now housed the Kilpatricks, jewellers, of Hillington.

"Jeanie Lumsden says they've shops in all the big towns," said Mrs. Cameron, "but the biggest is in Hillington. Fair fu' o' diamonds, so it is, just like Aladdin's cave. Could you believe it? Mr. Nigel's running the big Hillington shop now, for old Mr. Kilpatrick has the notion to retire in a year or two. Mr. Nigel's a young chap, and very handsome, though Jeanie says he fancies himself, but Jeanie could find fault with her own pinkie. She's my cousin, and whiles I couldn't thole her when we were wee."

"What about Mrs. Kilpatrick?" asked Merry, all agog to hear about her fascinating neighbours.

"Dead, poor sowl," said Mrs. Cameron, solemnly. "There's a daughter, too . . . Miss Stephanie, and she's a right young madam, though she works for the firm too. She's very smart, but you wouldna call her bonny, if you know what I mean."

Merry had a fair idea what she meant, though "bonny" often covered a variety of descriptions from pretty to plump.

"And what about Mr. Brendan?" she asked, curiously. "How long has he been here?"

"Just about a year—not long after your last holiday. Though, of course, he's no stranger, like the rest. He was supposed to be here on holiday, but he just stayed. Och, but he's a one, I must say." There was a faint softening in Mrs. Cameron's manner. "He once stopped by and asked if he could have my hands for a wee while." She spread out the strong, roughened fingers. "I was just to keep peeling my vegetables, and he'd sketch them. Dear knows how it turned out, for he never thocht to let me see. He's a funny one, but there's a gentleness to him, too, for I've seen him calm a frightened dog, and he even risked his hands, once, to help his wee cat when it got stuck after Kilpatrick's dog chased it up a tree. His hands are very sensitive, you see, so that he can use his brush skilfully. He used to have to get Joe Weir to chop wood for him in case he got blisters."

"Really?" commented Merry, interested.

"Aye, your Aunt Ellen was fond of him, and he was often over here at Beau Ness. I've had the job of cooking for him many a time."

Now Merry craned her neck as she came within sight of the Cot House. She'd have liked to ask Mrs. Cameron if she had any message for Mr. Brendan, but she knew better. She mustn't appear a forward young lady, or she'd be falling in Mrs. Cameron's estimation!

The Cot House looked like a tea-cosy with a riotous but colourful garden, and a warmth and friendliness which was very appealing. Merry's steps slowed and she stood on tip-toes to peer over the hedge.

"You'll see a lot more from this side," an amused voice informed her.

"Oh!"

Merry flushed scarlet as a tall and rather untidy-looking man rose from a rustic seat in the garden and regarded her with steady dark eyes. He wore stained blue jeans and a rust-coloured jersey with a hole in the front. His hair was slightly ruffled, but had been well cut, and the traditional bearded artist appearance was missing. Merry judged him to be around thirty, and felt taken aback because he looked so ordinary. She had been much too influenced by Mrs. Cameron's description of him as a "funny" one, though she should have known better. Mrs. Cameron used "funny" to describe as many things as she used "bonny".

Yet now she was finding herself the object of his scrutiny, and a flush stained her cheeks.

"Miss Merry Saunders," he said, "new owner of Beau Ness and goddaughter to Miss Ellen Blayne who was one of the sweetest ladies I ever knew. Good bones and colouring, and quite good expression if you like a shy fawn coming out of the woods. Won't you step into my parlour for a moment, and we'll introduce ourselves properly over a brew-up?"

"No, thank you," said Merry primly. "I really haven't time. I . . ."

"Haven't time? In Kilbraggan? What could you be doing which can't spare fifteen minutes? We've got to meet each other some time."

Merry felt his gaze mocking her, and bit her lip. Benjamin Brendan made her feel like a gauche schoolgirl caught stealing apples. Swiftly her chin rose.

"Very well, Mr. Brendan, I shall be pleased to drink tea with you."

With quiet dignity she opened the gate and he showed her into a living-room which made her eyes widen with interest. It seemed as though the room had been divided into two distinct sections. At one end he had a long table drawn up so that the long low window was directly behind it. Bookcases full of reference books lined the walls, and in a corner stood a large filing cabinet. The remainder of the room was furnished with comfortable armchairs, lovely old rugs and well-polished furniture.

"It's very . . . tidy," she said, a frank note of surprise in her voice. "One thinks of an artist as . . . well . . ."

"A dirty, untidy creature who throws paint on the floor and wipes his brush on the cat," suggested Benjamin, his dark eyes glittering with amusement. "Let's hope all your ideas aren't so firmly fixed, little Miss Merry." He picked up an electric kettle and began to fill it in the small kitchenette. "Commercial artists have to be surprisingly methodical, and we need lots of files for reference. I mean, suppose I were doing a cartoon strip and I find that jungle natives have killed a Kongoni. What is a Kongoni, and what does it look like? Maybe I ought to know, but quite often I don't. So I look it up."

"I see," said Merry, interested in spite of herself. "So you do cartoons."

"Cartoons, book jackets, children's annuals, magazine illustrations . . . whatever brings me in some bread and butter. And don't ask me if I ever try some *real* art, or I shall want to strangle you, Miss Merry. I'm not ashamed of being commercial, and I might dispute that any one form of art is any greater than another. My African native's hand needs as much care in drawing as . . . as . . ."

"Mrs. Cameron's at the vegetables," suggested Merry, and he shouted with laughter and lifted down a detective novel entitled *With These Hands.*

Merry grinned as she recognised Mrs. Cameron's white enamel bowl and strong fingers grasping a carrot.

"No wonder you never let her see it," she commented, handing back the book, "and don't keep calling me Miss Merry!"

"Merry, then, and I'm Benjamin. Not Benny. Benjamin."

"Benjamin," she agreed, accepting a piece of fruit cake with her steaming hot mug of strong tea.

"Who keeps house for you?" she asked, biting into the cake.

Benjamin gave her a cool look.

"Who else but myself?" he asked, squatting down beside her on an ample pouffe. "I've been my own master since my grandfather died, and I've learned how to live alone, and like it. Once or twice I might have been tempted to change that happy state of affairs . . . though I usually manage to resist temptation!"

He drank his tea, his eyes twinkling, and she felt again that he was laughing at her.

"Joe Weir and his wife come along three times a week and keep my house in order, when Joe hasn't a taxi job. But that's enough about me, Merry Saunders. What about you? What do you intend to do with yourself in a quiet place like Kilbraggan?"

Merry considered before answering. Her efforts at writing were still fairly new to her and rather precious. She hadn't yet grown tough enough to take all criticism, and her rejection slips often hurt for longer than they need. She couldn't bear it if this professional artist, used to doing book jackets for professional writers, laughed at her efforts. But as she looked into his strong square face, the broad forehead, the firm mouth, and the eyes bright and alert, she felt that he might understand.

"Well, do I pass?" he asked softly, and she laughed and coloured rosily.

"I hesitate to tell you, but I want to write."

"What kind of writing?"

"Oh, various things . . . short stories, articles, and I would like to try a novel."

"Then I can only wish you every success and hope you will still speak to me when you're famous."

Merry coloured angrily, feeling that he was laughing at her again.

"I must go," she said, rising swiftly, then hesitated, feeling that she was being rather abrupt.

"Thank you for the tea and cake. Perhaps you would come over for a meal one evening soon?"

"Next Wednesday," said Benjamin promptly. "It's the day I send off my weekly cartoon series, and I'll be free in the evening. Drop in when you want someone to talk to, though my guess is that you'll soon have plenty of friends."

"Who, for instance?" asked Merry curiously. "Is there a busy social life in the village?"

"You'll see," promised Benjamin, ushering her through the solid front door. "Cheerio, little Merry."

She turned to wave and watched him shut the door, then stepped out into the road, only to leap back again as a low white Jaguar turned the corner and pulled to a stop.

Merry saw that the driver was a fair young man, beautifully groomed in spite of being slightly windblown. Beside him sat a beautiful girl, so like him that she could be his twin sister. Her elaborately-styled hair was protected by a silk scarf, but her vivid blue eyes, set in near-perfect features, regarded Merry coolly as the driver came round to talk to her.

"It's a girl!" he said, steadying her with a strong delicate hand. "I thought I'd run over a wood nymph."

"I . . . I thought this was a private road," she said shakily.

"It is," drawled the girl. "If you're going to take all day, Nigel, I want a word with Benjamin."

"Go ahead, Stephanie. I suspect this is Miss Saunders, our new neighbour, and I want to get acquainted. I'm Nigel Kilpatrick, and this is my sister Stephanie."

"H . . . How do you do," said Merry shakily, while Stephanie acknowledged her with a cool nod, and strolled up to the front door of the Cot House, which opened suddenly.

"Well," said Benjamin, his eyes gleaming with amusement as he looked at all three, "it took less time than I thought, Merry." His eyes sobered as they rested on the lovely girl on the doorstep. "Hello, Stephanie. Am I being honoured with a visit?"

"Of course, darling," she said, smiling sweetly. "I expect Nigel will want to take Miss . . . er . . . home after nearly knocking her down. He can pick me up on the way past."

Again Benjamin's eyes glinted with amusement as he watched Nigel ceremoniously help Merry into the car.

"Come in, then, do," he said, opening the door wide. "Two charming visitors in one day. Truly more than one could hope for."

"Sorry about that, Miss Saunders," said Nigel, as the car swung out again into the main road.

"How did you know about me?" asked Merry, curiously.

"Local grapevine, of course," said Nigel. "Our cleaning woman is related to the worthy Mrs. Cameron."

"Of course," said Merry, chuckling a little. "Jeanie Lumsden. Hi, Mr. Kilpatrick, you've passed Beau Ness."

"I know. I thought we'd just go for a quick spin up round the loch to give Stephanie time to talk to Benjamin. And please call me Nigel, and I shall call you Merry."

He turned to grin at her, and Merry found her heart beating more quickly than usual, and bit her lip to control her quick breathing. She was behaving like a schoolgirl, even failing to protest when this young man, a complete stranger, was high-handedly taking her for a spin in his car, beautiful though it was, entirely without her permission.

"You go too fast for me, Mr. Kilpatrick," she said coolly. "Please take me back home. Mrs. Cameron will wonder where I am."

Immediately he was contrite.

"I'm sorry, my dear. I was carried away, I'm afraid. It's very seldom that we have new . . . and beautiful . . . young ladies coming to stay at Kilbraggan. I suppose I just wanted to get acquainted as quickly as possible. Sorry I can't turn the car just yet . . . the road's too narrow."

She was silent for a moment.

"We shan't be long, I promise you," he told her briskly, without the teasing note of laughter in his voice. "And please don't let's get off on the wrong foot. I shall call you Miss Saunders if you'd prefer it . . . but Merry is so much nicer."

"All right," she laughed, "and I'd love a spin round the loch, if you're sure it won't take too long."

"Not long enough for me," said Nigel gaily, then turned to her more seriously as he saw her eyes cool again. "You must be a witch, Merry. I don't know what's happening to me today. I don't behave like this every time I meet an attractive girl, believe me. In fact, I'm quite a sobersides of a business man."

"Oh, look! Isn't it all beautiful?" breathed

Merry, as the car rounded a corner and Loch Braggan shimmered in pale sunshine through trees which were breathtaking in their variety of autumn shades. "I could swear some of those leaves were bright scarlet, and others are still emerald. Just look at them reflected in the loch! I've never stayed in Kilbraggan this late in autumn . . . I think it's even more beautiful than in summer."

"I know," said Nigel. "I've tried to paint it, but it only looked garish and artificial. I suppose Benjamin Brendan could make more of it, if he wanted to, that is. He's an odd sort of chap, preferring to draw kids' comics to . . . this . . ."

Merry didn't feel qualified to comment as the car snaked along the narrow loch-side road.

"You're a jeweller, I believe," she said, changing the subject, and Nigel nodded.

"Jewellery, watches, gold, silver and a few antiques. Are you interested in jewellery?"

"What woman isn't?" asked Merry. "I've never owned any, but I often look in shop windows, and admire."

"I shall still be at home tomorrow afternoon," said Nigel, as the car suddenly emerged into a broader road. "Come over for tea, and you can look at some nice pieces. We're having a private cocktail party soon for some of our special customers, in the showrooms above our largest shop in Hillington. It gives our customers a chance to see very special pieces of jewellery, worn by mannequins. It takes care and thought to decide which pieces we want to display, so I've brought them home for consideration."

"I'd love that," said Merry. "Thank you . . . Nigel. Goodness, are we home already?"

"It was a circular route. I wouldn't want to get on the wrong side of your Mrs. Cameron. Not at this stage," he added meaningly, and she felt her cheeks flush rosily, as she watched him wave carelessly before driving towards the Cot House.

It was only two hours since she had left home, but in those two hours the world seemed to have become a different place. She had met Benjamin Brendan, and had found it slightly irritating that he obviously considered her little more than a child, and one who was an amusement to him.

But Nigel had been different. An hour in his company and she felt that she was someone special, someone of importance. He had made her feel that she was not just someone to be regarded casually. Stephanie, though, hadn't given her much attention. She would have liked a friend in Kilbraggan, but obviously it wasn't going to be Stephanie Kilpatrick.

As she opened the front door, a thought struck her. Why should a girl like Stephanie so obviously wish to cultivate Benjamin Brendan? He was fairly well-known, but not the sort of famous artist one would think could appeal to a girl like that.

27

"She's in love with him," thought Merry, as she quietly hung up her coat and went to find Mrs. Cameron.

After dinner, she found a book and sat down in front of the living-room fire, feeling suddenly exhausted. An hour or two later, Mrs. Cameron found her nodding, heavy-eyed, and ordered her up to bed.

"You must have a good rest, Miss Merry," she said briskly. "We'll leave everything else till tomorrow."

CHAPTER 2

NEXT morning Merry woke up feeling more rested than she had for months. Downstairs she found Mrs. Cameron busy in the big kitchen with its wonderful view of deep purple hills behind the colourful autumn trees.

"Och, you should have stayed in bed, Miss Merry," Mrs. Cameron told her. "I was just going to bring you a wee bit of breakfast on a tray."

"Never, unless I'm ill," Merry told her. "I hate breakfast in bed. I'd much rather have it here by the kitchen fire."

"Well . . ." Mrs. Cameron eyed her doubtfully, then drew up a chair to the table, deftly setting out breakfast crockery.

"I suppose you'll want to see over the house, Miss Merry," she said. "After all, it's yours now, and you'll want to see that everything is in order."

"It feels strange that it should be mine," Merry told her candidly. "I feel as though Aunt Ellen has just slipped out for a moment. I don't feel that it all belongs to me yet."

"Och, that will come in time," the older woman told her. "I'm real glad to see you here, as a matter of fact. I couldna thole the place empty. I know you're not kith and kin to Miss Ellen, but there's a likeness between the pair of you. I like fine to see you here. I was feart it would all get into other hands when Miss Ellen died."

Mrs. Cameron paused to give her nose a quick wipe, then briskly cleared away Merry's porridge plate and put a large dish of eggs and bacon before her.

"Oh, goodness!" gasped Merry.

"Eat it up, do," she was told. "You look like a wee orphan, all skin and bones. It's time somebody looked after you properly!"

Merry found the task surprisingly easy, and after breakfast she accompanied Mrs. Cameron round the old cottage. The sitting-room was lovely, with fine, well-polished furniture and charmingly faded carpets and curtains. At the far end was an archway which led into a tiny room furnished with a large desk, two comfortable chairs and multiple bookshelves. A long low window gave a lovely view of the garden at the side of the cottage.

Merry had rarely sat in Aunt Ellen's study, except to write now and again, as the older woman had considered it a private domain, and now she wandered round, looking at it all with pleasure. The pale leaf green carpet blended beautifully with gold brocade curtains and pretty cretonne covers for the chairs. She loved the atmosphere of the tiny room, and felt she could work well here.

"I won't disturb you in here, Miss Merry," Mrs. Cameron was telling her. "Miss Ellen liked it that way, too, and if you don't want to be disturbed by callers, then you can always be out."

"Thank you, Mrs. Cameron," laughed Merry.

"Can we go upstairs now? I put you in Miss Ellen's bedroom, but moved your things."

"Yes, I saw. Thank you, Mrs. Cameron. It ... it was very thoughtful of you."

"It will seem like your own room in no time," the older woman comforted her. "This is a friendly house, and has always given succour to its owner. There's been no sadness or evil here in living memory, and nothing but good tales are told of the place."

"I know. I'm sensitive to atmosphere," said Merry, climbing the old polished stairs. "It was always a happy house to me, and I loved staying with Aunt Ellen."

Together they inspected the three bedrooms and tiny boxroom.

"Will you want to see my rooms?" asked Mrs. Cameron diffidently, and Merry assured her that she didn't, so long as she was quite satisfied.

The bathroom was new and luxurious in pale aquamarine tiles with deeper green fittings. Ellen Blayne had loved green, saying it was nature's own colour, and she certainly hadn't skimped when it came to her new bathroom. However, Merry felt happy with her choice, and delighted Mrs. Cameron by admiring its immaculate appearance. The day before she had still been too tired to take it all in.

Back downstairs, Mrs. Cameron indicated a small table covered with notebooks and papers.

"Will you look through these, Miss Merry?" she asked. "They were in a small chest of drawers Miss Ellen decided to give to an old lady in the village. She went to see her when she was ill, and found the puir sowl had nowhere to keep her claes."

Merry picked up the notebooks and leafed through them.

"Miss Ellen took ill after that," Mrs. Cameron told her, "and couldna attend to them hersel', so I kept them. I didn't want to burn them till you saw them."

Already Merry was reading the small, neat

writing, turning the pages with interest. They had been written when Aunt Ellen was young, in the nineteen-twenties, and something at the back of Merry's mind was responding to the small gay snippets of nonsense they contained. Already the whole personality of Ellen Blayne, whom she'd loved so dearly, was catching her imagination.

"I'd like all this put in the study, Mrs. Cameron," she said, "I'd like to go through them all at my leisure. Oh, that reminds me, I shall be going out this afternoon."

"Oh, aye?" asked Mrs. Cameron inquiringly, and Merry hesitated for a moment.

"Mr. Kilpatrick has invited me over to Rossie House," she explained, "for tea, and to show me some of his jewellery."

"Oh, aye," said Mrs. Cameron again, this time with a small non-committal nod.

"Oh, and Mr. Brendan, the artist, is coming to tea next Wednesday."

"Oh, aye," said Mrs. Cameron for the third time, and a gleam lit her eyes. "Seems like we're getting to know the neighbours, Miss Merry. Not that Mr. Brendan is a stranger, you might say. He is and he isn't. We all ken wha he is, if you get my meaning."

"I don't," said Merry, bewildered.

"Why, he's a Ross-Findlater, and is really the last of them, now Mr. Ian and old Mr.

Alexander have both gone. Miss Alison married Mark Brendan of Ladykirk, you see, and when Mr. Ian died, there was only the old man left at Rossie House, and Mr. Benjamin still at school. Davie Laird was at the Cot House in them days, to see to things. Then old Mr. Ross-Findlater died, and last year Davie Laird followed him, puir sowl, and Mr. Benjamin decided to come home. He's the real owner of Rossie House, Miss Merry, only he's rented it to the Kilpatricks."

"Oh, I see," said Merry.

There was no need to wonder any longer why Stephanie Kilpatrick so obviously wanted Benjamin Brendan. His must be one of the oldest families in the neighbourhood.

"He'll be right welcome here, Miss Merry," said Mrs. Cameron. "He called a few times to see Miss Ellen, but latterly she wasn't so well and couldn't entertain much. She aye liked him, though."

"I thought you said he was a funny one."

"So he is," defended Mrs. Cameron. "He makes me laugh, the way he goes on."

Mrs. Cameron again told her all about Benjamin's behaviour in public, punctuated with hearty giggles.

"Mr. Kilpatrick seems nice," put in Merry softly, remembering Nigel's dancing blue eyes and charming smile.

"Oh, aye," said Mrs. Cameron non-committally. "Yon Miss Stephanie is chasing Mr. Benjamin at the moment, and she'll have him, too, if he doesn't watch out. She's fair spoiled, that girl. She once condescended to help with a garden party for church funds, and Mrs. Cairns, the minister's wife, asked her to help me sell home provisions, and I was never so near slapping any young girl, she was that uppity and bossy. If you ask me, it's what she's short of, and another one I could name, too, and that's Miss Sylvia. I was always glad when she didn't stay here long, and that's a fact. Folk don't know how to bring up girls these days."

"No?" asked Merry, grinning.

"I wasn't meaning you, as you well know," said Mrs. Cameron. "It's been the opposite for you, and you could do with a bit of spoiling now. Only mind the Kilpatricks, Miss Merry. They're strangers, you see."

"But I thought they'd been here almost a year."

"Still strangers," said Mrs. Cameron firmly, "and it doesn't do for a young man to have a conceit of himself. Och, never mind an old woman's havers," she added, as she saw Merry's puzzled face. "Go and have a good time. I'll get a nice bit of salmon for Mr. Benjamin's tea."

After lunch Merry dressed carefully in her best suit of russet-coloured tweed, beautifully

34

cut to enhance her neat figure. She brushed her soft brown hair till it shone with red lights, and applied discreet make-up. Satisfied with her appearance, she went downstairs and into the kitchen.

"I don't expect I'll be home late, Mrs. Cameron."

The older woman turned, then gasped with delight.

"My, but you look a fair treat, Miss Merry," she said admiringly. "I didn't realise you were such a braw lass."

Merry dimpled at the compliment, and was grateful for it. It gave her poise and confidence, and she felt well able to deal with Stephanie, if she happened to be at home. Nigel had made no mention of who else was likely to be present when she went to tea, but Merry felt full of eager anticipation as she walked lightly down the road in her neat leather shoes, polished like chestnuts. It was a lovely autumn day with only a soft breeze to rustle the trees and send a scattering of leaves down to swirl gently round her feet. Merry tried to catch one, as Mrs. Cameron had promised her a happy year ahead if she could, but found it surprisingly difficult.

Passing the Cot House, she glanced at the windows, but saw no sign of life. The narrow road twisted between trees for about a hundred yards, then widened into the courtyard in front of Rossie House. It was a charming old place, 'surprisingly small and neat, with sash windows peeping through ivy, and neat flower beds beside the gravel path.

Merry walked up to the heavy front door, passing Nigel's white Jaguar sports car, and pulled the bell. An elderly woman with an inquisitive face, neat grey hair and a plain black dress opened the door. Merry had no difficulty in recognising Jeanie Lumsden.

"I'm Miss Saunders," she said. "Mr. Nigel Kilpatrick invited me for tea.".

"Come in, you're expectit," the woman nodded. "I'll tell Mr. Nigel you're here."

She showed Merry into a small room off the hall, while from behind another door Merry could hear the sound of voices talking animatedly. The housekeeper took little notice of this, however, and knocked loudly on the door before opening it.

"Miss Saunders's here, Mr. Nigel," she announced.

"I'll come now, Jeanie."

"Who?" asked another voice.

"The new young girl at Beau Ness, Miss Blayne's niece. I asked her over for tea."

Merry could hear the deeper voice rumbling again, then Nigel spoke.

"We'll talk about this later, Father, but I still say it's worth the risk. If the first one's a success then we should do another, even if it's after

Christmas. We must keep presenting something new, even in jewellery. We . . ."

Again the voice faded a little, then a door slammed and Nigel was pushing open the door of the small room.

"Merry! How nice of you to come. Come through to the study and meet my father."

Merry rose a trifle uncertainly, then smiled and nodded.

"Thank you, Nigel, I'd love to."

Mr. Kilpatrick was a heavily-built man, in his late fifties, with neat grey hair and tired eyes. He rose and whipped off a pair of spectacles, to which an extra eye-glass had been fixed, before shaking Merry's hand.

"Come and sit down, my dear," he said, indicating a comfortable leather armchair.

The study was a large room, full of books, chairs and small tables, but mainly dominated by the large desk behind which Mr. Kilpatrick now sat. To one side were several rolls of thin leather material, and Mr. Kilpatrick reached for one and unrolled it on top of the desk.

"Nigel tells me you're interested in seeing some of our special pieces of jewellery," he said, genially. "What do you think of this?"

Merry gasped as he lifted back the velvet flaps, and showed a large range of diamond brooches.

"Sit over here at the desk, Merry," said Nigel,

pulling up a chair. "I knew you'd love to see these."

The next hour was one of the most exciting Merry had known. She was allowed to handle wonderful diamond brooches, exquisitely designed and set with perfectly matched stones.

"How beautiful!" she gasped, as Nigel picked up a lovely rose, entirely encrusted with diamonds.

"Here it is in rubies and diamonds," said Mr. Kilpatrick, picking up another.

"It's like a wonderful fairy tale," said Merry, and watched while Mr. Kilpatrick unrolled another leather roll, to show her a selection of gold bracelets, some in heavy figured gold, and some again set with diamonds, rubies and sapphires.

"You haven't many emeralds," she commented.

"We've quite a few among the rings," Nigel told her, opening a fitted case and drawing out some ring pads. "They're scarce now, though, and a flawless emerald is even more costly than a diamond. They're a very brittle stone, you know, and easily broken. What do you think of that one?"

Merry gasped as he picked out a large square-cut emerald, surrounded by diamonds.

"It's . . . magnificent!" she said, awed.

"And this diamond one," went on Mr. Kilpatrick, "might interest you. It's been designed so that several cuts of diamonds have been used, brilliant cut, marquise, baguette, round that lovely pear-shaped stone in the centre."

It was plain that both men were very knowledgeable about their gems, and Merry felt free to ask as many questions as she liked. She gazed, fascinated, while Mr. Kilpatrick pointed out the various cuts in stones and showed her why a beautiful clear solitaire is always more expensive than three lesser stones.

"You may be interested in this," said Mr. Kilpatrick, lifting up a leather case and flicking back the lid. Inside were several large shapes, made of clear plastic. "This is a replica of a rough diamond (much larger, of course), and shows how it crystallises in the cubic system. This next one shows how the diamond can be sawn into two, and the next one shows how it begins to be polished into a brilliant cut stone, such as you know it. Here you see how the facets are formed, and here, finally, is the replica of a perfectly polished diamond, with fifty-eight facets. It's the hardest substance in the world, and when you buy a diamond, it's for ever."

"But how is it polished if there's nothing harder?" asked Merry.

A gleam came into the older man's eyes.

"With diamond, my dear. Only diamond can polish diamond. Rubies and sapphires are corundum, and are the same stones, only different colours. They're not so hard as diamonds, of course. This beautiful pale blue stone is a zircon, but it's much softer. White zircon is sometimes mistaken for diamond, though it hasn't the same fire when you see them side by side."

"And turquoise?" asked Merry, picking up a gold brooch whose flower petals were studded with lovely blue turquoise, the heart of the flower set with diamonds.

"They're phosphate," said Nigel. "They're found with limonite, and the finest blue turquoise comes from Khorasan in Persia. Green is more common, but not such good stones."

Merry sat back in her chair, and gazed again at the glittering array. The final roll contained necklaces and ear-rings, some of which matched brooches and rings she'd already seen.

"And . . . and do you always keep these in the house?" she asked, rather fearfully.

"Goodness, no," laughed Nigel. "Normally you'd have to come to the shop in Hillington, which is our biggest, or several shops even. This is a special occasion, when we have gathered this large stock together. Next Saturday we are having a private cocktail party in the showrooms above the Hillington shop, as I believe I mentioned to you, and we want to decide what the mannequins will wear. This pink topaz ring will, I think, be the *pièce de résistance*."

Merry gasped again as Nigel lifted a small blue leather ring case, and threw back the lid.

Inside lay a beautiful ring, a huge stone glittering with pink fire.

"That's our most expensive ring at the moment, because of its rarity," he explained. "Topaz are good gemstones and this one is forty carats, and its clarity and cut are faultless. Stephanie will wear this one, also the diamond necklace and tiara."

"She'll look . . . wonderful," said Merry, in an awed voice, then put the ring down quickly. For a moment she felt slightly giddy, and rather cold and shivery as she looked at the ring, but the feeling passed quickly and she admired its great beauty.

"Wouldn't you like to come to the cocktail party?" Nigel asked her. "I'm sure you'd enjoy it."

Her eyes glowed as Mr. Kilpatrick nodded and smiled, his long sensitive fingers busy with the leather rolls, folding back the velvet, rolling them up and tying them neatly with blue cord.

"Why not?" he asked.

"I'd love to," she said shyly. "I've never been to anything like that in my life."

"We may be having another after Christmas, in one of the big hotels. I thought jewellery and furs, if the furrier I know agrees . . . and if Father agrees."

He grinned slyly at Mr. Kilpatrick.

"I'll wait and see how this one goes, Nigel," he said, a note of decision in his voice. "I'm still not convinced that parties of this kind are the best way of selling our goods. Our business has been built up, slowly, over the years, on trust and on satisfying old and valued customers who wouldn't want to enjoy some of your smart new ideas."

"And I say it's ridiculous not to try them out for that reason," said Nigel, and Merry was surprised to see how different he looked when decisive. The pleasant, boyish face looked grim, then he caught her eye, and laughed merrily.

"Sorry, my dear," he apologised. "Dad and I often air our views, as though we were ready to fight each other. You'll have to get used to the Kilpatrick temperament."

A moment later Jeanie Lumsden knocked loudly on the door to say she'd served tea in the lounge.

"Then we'd better go and eat, my dear," said Mr. Kilpatrick. "Why isn't Stephanie here?"

Stephanie, however, didn't appear until they were all seated round the fine oval table, and Merry was pouring tea from a large silver pot.

"Sorry I'm late," she apologised, sauntering into the lounge, and stopping to stare at Merry.

"I think you've met before," said Nigel, politely. "Miss Saunders from Beau Ness ... my sister Stephanie."

The older girl took in Merry's neat suit and well-groomed appearance, then smiled a trifle coolly.

"Well, well, we are getting matey," she said, sliding into a chair. "May I have a cup of tea, too?"

"Of course," said Merry calmly, passing it over. "I've just been admiring your wonderful stock of jewellery, Miss Kilpatrick."

"Yes, it is rather nice, isn't it?" said Stephanie.

"We've invited Merry to the cocktail party," Nigel told her.

Stephanie weighed her up lazily, then nodded.

"Good," she said. "She could be quite a lot of help. By the way, I called in to see Benjamin, Daddy, and he agrees to those alterations. I believe you've met our landlord, Miss Saunders —Benjamin Brendan?"

"We met the other day," said Merry. "He invited me in for tea."

"Yes, he's inclined to be anxious about people. I'm afraid I worry about him a little. We're . . . good friends, you know."

Stephanie gazed directly at the younger girl, and Merry could not fail to get the message. She was being warned off. Stephanie was willing to accept her, though she was probably too big a snob to treat her as a bosom friend, so long as she made no effort to attract Benjamin. Merry could have laughed aloud at the idea. She glanced across at Nigel, and had to admit that he was very attractive, though she would have to guard her heart carefully against him, as it

43

was unlikely he would fall in love with an ordinary girl like her. He must meet beautiful and glamorous girls every day.

"Do you like Beau Ness?" Mr. Kilpatrick was asking. "It's a fine solid little house."

"Rather quaint," said Stephanie sweetly. "How big is it?"

"Six rooms, then kitchen quarters and two extra rooms for Mrs. Cameron," said Merry. "Aunt Ellen loved it, and so do I."

"But she wasn't your real aunt, was she?" asked Stephanie. "I understood you're an orphan."

"My mother was at school with Aunt Ellen . . . Hilsden, actually, and I went there myself until a few years ago. Daddy was a missionary, but he died . . ."

"Not Gregory Saunders?" broke in Mr. Kilpatrick, and eyed Merry with respect when she nodded. "I've read some of his essays and articles, my dear. He has inspired me many times. You must be proud of him."

"I am," said Merry gratefully, and rather shakily.

"I've asked Benjamin for tea on Wednesday, but he says he has a previous engagement," said Stephanie loudly, obviously bored with the subject. "Whatever could he be doing that's so important?"

Merry bit her lip, hoping the sudden colour in her cheeks didn't give her away.

"Perhaps I'd better be getting home," she said, rising rather abruptly. "Mrs. Cameron and I are busy sorting out Aunt Ellen's things."

"I'll drive you home," offered Nigel.

"No, it's all right . . . I'd like to walk."

"Then I'll walk with you. It will probably do us both good."

As they passed the Cot House, the crimson and pink streamers from the setting sun lighting it up with a vivid glow, Merry caught sight of Benjamin hanging over the gate.

"Good evening," he grinned at both of them. "Wonderful night for walking."

"It certainly is," agreed Nigel with enthusiasm, and Merry wondered why she felt slightly annoyed when he tucked her hand possessively through his arm. She wriggled uncomfortably, feeling as though Benjamin's eyes were boring through her back, then laughed at her own imagination. What an irritating effect Benjamin had on her, she thought crossly.

As they reached the gates of Beau Ness, Nigel refused an invitation to come in, but clasped Merry's hand warmly, then bent and quickly kissed her cheek.

"You're a lovely girl, Merry," he whispered. "Goodnight, my dear . . . see you soon."

"Goodnight, Nigel," said Merry softly.

That night she wanted to dream of Nigel, but his blue in his friendly boyish face refused to stay in her mind. Instead it was Benjamin who grinned at her sardonically, and Merry fell asleep still feeling cross with herself.

CHAPTER 3

ON Wednesday Benjamin turned up for tea looking spruce in a brown tweed suit and fawn woollen tie. Merry was still getting used to the Scottish high tea which Mrs. Cameron preferred to serve, and which she, too, was beginning to prefer.

It was obvious that Benjamin preferred it, too, as Mrs. Cameron greeted him with the news that tea wouldn't be long. She had a nice bit of salmon she was serving up with two kinds of salads, and her scones would soon be out of the oven.

"Good," said Benjamin, rubbing his hands as he sat down in front of the sitting-room fire while Merry excused herself for a moment and ran to repair her make-up. When she returned, wearing a clover-pink angora dress, he looked very much at home with his long legs stretched out comfortably.

"I like this room," he remarked. "It's got the right atmosphere. I could paint you one day, sitting on this chair here. Come and see what you look like."

Obediently she came to sit beside him on the chair he indicated, and he pretended to study her from all angles.

"Very nice," he approved, and Merry found herself blushing like a schoolgirl.

"I'm glad you're satisfied," she said, a trifle tartly.

"Tell me what you've been doing with yourself, apart from trotting up to Rossie House," he commanded, and again Merry coloured a little.

"I only went to tea," she said defensively, "and to see some of their jewellery, though I don't expect you'd be interested in that."

"Why not?" asked Benjamin. "Of course I'm interested. In fact, I'm going tomorrow night to photograph some of it for a new book cover I'm working on. It's called *The Seven Diamonds Mystery*, and I expect Stephanie to find me at least seven diamonds."

"Are you being sarcastic?" asked Merry, and some of the laughter left his eyes.

"I'm sorry you think that, Merry. In fact, I've no particularly strong feelings about the undoubted fine pieces of jewellery the Kilpatricks sell. I just can't help remembering, at times, that one of their fine choice rings could provide quite a few dinners for the McConnells, and old Jake Grieve could not only have a new pair of boots, but a whole new wardrobe of clothes with the change."

"You can't compare the two," defended Merry. "The fact that hundreds of people are poor and ill-fed doesn't mean that beautiful jewellery should not be made, jewellery which will last for ever. And in any case, I've seen the McConnells tucking into some good rabbit stew and apple pie, and Jake's new boots, when he gets them, will give him even more pleasure than a new bracelet would give to a wealthy woman."

There was a gentle knock on the door.

"Will you be coming now for your tea?" asked Mrs. Cameron. "I've laid it all ready in the dining-room, and I've lit the fire, Miss Merry. The days are a bit chilly now."

"Lovely, Mrs. Cameron," smiled Merry. "Shall we go, then, Benjamin?"

It was a cosy tea, but Merry felt very conscious of the strong-natured man sitting across the table.

"Have you started writing yet?" he asked bluntly.

She hesitated before replying, and Benjamin pursed his lips.

"I shouldn't like to think you were one of those people who talk plenty about writing, but are so busy talking they've no time for doing."

"Of course I'm not," protested Merry. "As a matter of fact, I've been busy making notes. I've found lots of notebooks belonging to Aunt Ellen and they've given me an idea for a book. They capture the atmosphere of the twenties so vividly, and I've found plenty of photographs and things like theatre programmes."

She warmed to her subject, and was unaware how attractive she looked as her cheeks flushed and her eyes glowed.

"Aunt Ellen would make a wonderful heroine. I used to wonder why she hadn't married, because she was so lovely, but I think I know now. I think she was in love with a young man who was killed in a climbing accident . . . Ian Ross-Findlater."

"My uncle," put in Benjamin.

"Oh, I forgot," said Merry, a trifle taken aback.

"He was my godfather, and looked after me when my parents died. Grandfather was rather old, you see."

"I . . . I'm sorry," she said awkwardly, at a loss to express the sympathy she felt. "Perhaps I'd better not put him in the story . . . even if I disguise both of them quite a lot."

"Why not?" asked Benjamin. "Perhaps it would make them happy to have their love story handed down to posterity."

"There you go again," said Merry with annoyance. "You always seem to be laughing at me!"

Benjamin's black eyes regarded her thoughtfully.

"It was meant to be a gently teasing remark," he told her. "I think you're far too sensitive about your writing, Merry. You mustn't fly off the handle at perfectly innocent comments. I don't know what your writing is like, but I remember Miss Blayne telling me you'd sold some of your stuff, so at least the potential is there, and I trust you are intelligent and tenacious enough to develop it. So for goodness' sake stop looking for insults, and try to believe I'm taking an intelligent interest in you."

"Are you?" she asked, and his face softened into a smile at her look of wide-eyed innocence.

"Of course I am," he assured her. "I promised your Aunt Ellen I'd look after you, and that's a promise I intend to keep."

"Oh."

Merry felt slightly taken aback, then she looked at Benjamin with new understanding of the slightly bossy attitude he used towards her, which irritated her so much. He felt responsible for her, because he had promised Aunt Ellen!

"I'm old enough to look after myself," she told him tartly, and again his eyes lit with amusement.

"Of course you are," he agreed placatingly. "Now, if we can go back to Uncle Ian. I'll find out all I can about him for you, if you think it will help."

"Thank you," she said mechanically, still feeling ruffled inside. The last thing she wanted was a watch-dog!

But when Benjamin left for home, after tea,

and waved to her casually from the gate, she watched his tall figure swinging down the road until he was out of sight.

The showrooms above Kilpatricks at Hillington still showed signs of last-minute preparations, when Merry arrived with Nigel. Stephanie had asked if she would like to help to keep a check on the stock as Mr. Kilpatrick's secretary had just left to get married, and Stephanie was to have taken her place.

"Here's a list of the goods on each stand," she said, handing Merry a typewritten list, "and here's the most important one, a list of our largest pieces to be worn by the mannequins. There are six girls in all, five and myself. I'll wear the diamonds, and the final piece will be the topaz ring. I've got a black velvet evening dress for the diamonds, and a silver cocktail for the ring. I'll show you the changing room, then you can collect the pieces and return them to Nigel where you'll both initial the list after he has locked them in the case. O.K.?"

"O.K.," said Merry, rather nervously, feeling dazzled by her surroundings. Six stands had been set up in one end of the room, and members of Kilpatricks' staff were busy laying out jewellery on the crimson velvet pads. One stand was devoted to cultured pearls and artificial grass had been used as a background for their wonderful milky-white texture. Another stand was

51

entirely devoted to antique jewellery, and Merry was fascinated by the heavy, rather ornate pieces, her imagination stirred by the ghosts of gracious ladies of a bygone age, wearing these very pieces at glittering social occasions.

"You've got an awful lot of stock," she said to Stephanie.

"Not quite so much as this," the other girl told her. "Some of the London manufacturers who supply our stocks have kindly sent us extra pieces especially for this evening. These cocktail rings, for instance, have been lent, as few people in Hillington buy cocktail rings at the moment and it's helpful to show them what is available. It might create a demand."

Merry examined the tray of large, gem-studded rings, some designed like flowers, and watched while a smart young lady slipped them into individual pads, and placed them attractively on the stand.

"They look fabulous to me," she whispered.

She glanced at her list.

"Those are stock numbers," Stephanie pointed out. "You'll find a small ticket on each piece, and it will have that number written on it in red ink. On the other side, in black ink, is the price code. Sure you can read it, if asked?"

"Quite sure," nodded Merry. Nigel had spent some time teaching her this.

"Good," laughed Stephanie. "We'll make a jeweller of you yet!"

Merry coloured a little at the praise, glad that Stephanie appeared to have accepted her. The fair girl looked beautiful this evening, her lovely silvery blonde hair having been set in a criss-cross style, her cool delicate features artistically made-up.

Merry, too, was looking her best in a beautiful emerald green chiffon cocktail dress, expertly cut, with flowing panels down the back. Nigel had approved of it wholeheartedly when he called to collect her, and she was glad that Aunt Ellen had given her such good advice when choosing her clothes.

Her only adornment, apart from her gold watch, was the small scarlet disc which a detective had given her at the door. Everyone wore a similar disc, and each name had been ticked off as the disc was handed out.

"You'll see one or two solid-looking gentlemen mingling with the guests," Nigel told her, with a smile. "Don't lose your disc, or you're liable to be quietly removed. They've a good way of spotting anyone who's been clever enough to gatecrash."

"You've thought of everything," said Merry.

"We have to," Nigel told her grimly. "There's been so many jewel robberies, the insurance companies are getting sticky, and I don't blame them. If we're careless, they won't pay up if we lose anything."

Now Merry began to study her list, and to

help Nigel sort out the pieces for each mannequin to wear. Mr. Kilpatrick was welcoming his guests and showing them to small tables at the other end of the room, where discreet waiters were serving champagne, and bowls of crisps and nuts had been put in the centre of each table, together with cigarettes and ashtrays.

Merry had a moment to study the guests. Many of the women looked elegant and charming and were already wearing a lovely but discreet piece of jewellery. Their husbands, looking every inch the successful professional or business man, laughed and joked with Mr. Kilpatrick.

There were others, however, with sharp discontented faces and tired eyes, whose fingers were already clustered with glittering rings, while gold bracelets jostled each other on flabby white arms. Merry watched them weigh up the scene calculatingly, and shivered a little with distaste, as though a splash of ugliness had been painted over a lovely picture.

"New warm clothes for the McConnells and decent living conditions for some of the cottagers in Kilbraggan," whispered a voice in her ear.

Merry started, then smiled as she turned to find Benjamin grinning at her.

"Boots for Jake Grieve," she returned.

"He's got a pair," he told her.

"I didn't know you were coming."

"I made up my mind at the last moment," he told her smilingly. "See how the other half live.

54

Stephanie invited me." Proudly he displayed his red badge. "Are you enjoying yourself, little Merry?"

"I'm here to work," she told him proudly, folding her list.

"Nice working clothes. In that dress, your hair looks like lovely ripe chestnuts."

Merry couldn't stop the warm colour flooding her cheeks, though the compliment was made in such an indulgent tone that she knew she couldn't take it seriously.

"I'm glad you like it," she said primly; and he laughed.

"What sort of work?" he asked, looking round curiously.

"Checking," she told him. "I've been given a list of the jewellery to be shown, and I mark off each piece as I get it from the models."

Benjamin frowned.

"Whose idea was that?" he asked, rather coldly.

"Why, Stephanie's or Nigel's, I suppose. Does it matter?"

He looked at her thoughtfully.

"They've no right to ask you to take responsibility like this," he said firmly. "You're only a youngster, and there's thousands at stake in this little lot. If anything should go wrong . . . something missing, for example . . . it means you're involved."

She flushed scarlet.

"You . . . you aren't saying I can't be trusted?" she snapped, her eyes sparking. "Or that I'm some sort of incompetent fool? I've had a good office training, and I used to hold down quite a responsible job with my uncle's firm. Do you think the Kilpatricks would ask me if they thought I was some sort of idiot? I . . ."

"Steady on, steady on," he told her. "Don't keep flying off the handle because I talk a bit of horse sense to you. If you can't see the risk, then heaven help me, I must try to point it out to you . . ."

"Well, you can stop playing watchdog to me," she told him stormily. "Even if you did promise Aunt Ellen!"

"Why, Benjamin darling, I'm so glad you got here!"

Suddenly Stephanie was with them, darting Merry an angry look, and her heart sank even more. She had no wish to be bad friends with Stephanie. While she couldn't exactly foresee a bosom friendship between them, or a time when she'd be very fond of Stephanie, yet she was Nigel's sister, and Merry would have welcomed a girl of her own age as a friend. She'd felt that the other girl was beginning to like her a little, and was annoyed with Benjamin, quite illogically, for giving her the wrong impression.

"Where's Nigel?" asked Stephanie.

"Getting a quick cup of coffee," said Merry. "He'll be back in a moment. I've had mine."

"We need him, fast . . . Oh, here he is now. Nigel, Claire Turner hasn't turned up. Molly says she's caught the 'flu bug. That means no one for the turquoise and pearls."

"Oh, lord," exclaimed Nigel. "That puts the programme out. I suppose you can't . . . No, the timing would be wrong. Wait a minute . . . What about Merry?"

He eyed her emerald dress, and shook his head again.

"Molly could wear the turquoise," said Stephanie. "She's in cream silk, for the garnets. They'd look O.K. on Merry . . . quite vivid against the green."

They considered her speculatively, while Merry stood by uneasily, aware of Benjamin's tall figure in the background. .

"Will you do it, Merry?" asked Nigel.

"I . . . I don't know," she said, biting her lip as she caught Benjamin's stern face, as he stared angrily at Nigel. Then Stephanie made a gesture of impatience.

"Why not?" demanded Nigel. "You've got the looks, you're dressed properly, and you can walk. Why not, for goodness' sake?"

"She's too timid," sneered Stephanie, and Benjamin's eyes snapped.

"She's only a child, Kilpatrick," he interrupted. "You've no right to put responsibility on to her!"

Merry's chin came up.

"Of course I'll do it," she said crisply, "if you think I can. What about the checking, though?"

"I'll manage that myself," Nigel told her. "Dave Bruce will help. Go with Stephanie to the changing room and I'll be right along with the case."

As they walked away, Stephanie's fingers closed lightly on Merry's wrist, then firmed slightly as they passed one of the stands. Merry saw a very tall young man with dark curling hair and very dark eyes looking at Stephanie fixedly, and felt sudden tension in the girl.

"Who is that?" she asked curiously.

"One of our managers," the girl told her, and shrugged in an attempt to be offhand. "Does it matter?"

Merry had to admit that it didn't, though for a moment she had felt surrounded by tensions.

"Now, let's see your hair and make-up," Stephanie was saying. "Here's the other girls, Molly Green, Val Stoddart, Irene Price and Betty McArthur. Merry Saunders, girls . . . our neighbour at Kilbraggan. She'll take Claire's place, or at least your place, Molly. The garnets will look better on her dress, and the turquoise will be fine with that cream silk."

"Suits me," said Molly, with a friendly smile at Merry. "We're all enjoying the change from clothes. We all model at some of the big stores in town."

Merry nodded, feeling suddenly nervous

58

again. What if she made a fool of herself, with Nigel watching . . . and Benjamin. The thought made her chin firm, and she decided she wouldn't give him that satisfaction. She smiled as Nigel walked in the door carrying a black fitted jewel case, full of black leather-bound boxes.

"All right, girls," he said gently. "Here we are. Stephanie first, with the diamonds, then I think it's Irene with the sapphire necklace and matching bracelet."

Somehow or other it was Merry's turn, as she fastened on a heavy jewel-encrusted necklace, with bracelet, ear-rings and brooch to match. This was the only antique set in the collection, and she was very conscious of previous owners, as she walked up the centre of the floor, turning and twisting to allow the bright lights to catch the living fire of the jewels. The garnets glowed deep, rich red, so different from the bright pinkish crimson of the rubies worn by Betty. Merry felt the weight of them on her neck and arms, and decided that a whole evening wearing them was not for her.

It was with relief that she walked back to the changing room amid polite but quite enthusiastic applause, and gave the gems back to Nigel, who marked off each piece, had it checked by the tall young man with dark hair, and locked it away in the case.

By midnight it was all over, and Merry stood

waiting tiredly for Nigel and his father to lock everything away in huge safes, expertly fitted with burglar alarms.

"Has it been a success?" she asked, rather tiredly.

"Too soon to tell," said Nigel tersely. "Some people have made up their minds about things tonight, and one or two cocktail rings have been bought with a few gold animal brooches. Pearls, too!" He turned to carry more boxes to the safe. "The bigger pieces aren't bought so quickly. People like time to consider these things. Isn't that so, Father?"

Mr. Kilpatrick nodded.

"That's how it should be," he said. "Impulsive buying means a dissatisfied customer when the enthusiasm wanes. That's why I prefer ordinary business methods, but I'm willing to give Nigel his head this once. At least our stock checks, and we've no unpleasantness over that."

"Did no one buy the topaz ring?" asked Merry, and again felt herself shiver a little. Goose walking over her grave, she thought, a trifle uncomfortably.

"That will take a great deal of consideration," smiled Mr. Kilpatrick. "But someone will buy it, never fear. Thank you for your help, my dear. You filled the breach admirably."

"I enjoyed it," said Merry, then wondered if she was really being very truthful. It had been new and exciting, but now she wanted to be back home to Beau Ness, and Mrs. Cameron waiting for her with some hot milk. This wasn't really her world.

"Merry's tired," said Nigel, taking her arm possessively. "It's time I took you home, my love."

CHAPTER 4

MERRY enjoyed working at her desk in the lovely little study, off the sitting-room, while Mrs. Cameron hovered around like an anxious hen. At first she had been very conscious of the other woman's efforts to keep quiet, and told Mrs. Cameron to carry on normally, and she'd soon get used to her being there. Now she was into a good working routine, and filled with the intense urge which sometimes came to her when she was doing her best work.

In addition to reading through Aunt Ellen's notebooks, and making notes for her book, she wrote a short story, the words coming feverishly from an idea which had come to her during one of her solitary rambles through the woods. She was also preparing an article on the care of jewellery, and how to clean precious stones, and Nigel had promised to walk over with detailed information when he was free.

Now she put her short story into an envelope

with a wonderful feeling of satisfaction, and decided to walk down to the village to post it.

"Do you want anything from Maggie Scott's?" she asked Mrs. Cameron, knowing that she patronised the general stores.

"I'll see," Mrs. Cameron told her, bustling away to check her store cupboard. A few minutes later she was back with an old-fashioned shopping basket and a list of groceries.

"If you get these, Miss Merry," she said, "it'll save my legs tomorrow, and I can turn out the bedrooms instead."

"Couldn't I help you?" asked Merry, rather anxiously, thinking the older woman looked tired.

"Bless you, no," laughed Mrs. Cameron. "It'll be a funny day when I can't give the bedrooms a good redd. Och no, it's just that I was over at my sister's yesterday . . . her that lives in the village . . . you know, Isa and John Campbell."

Merry nodded. She'd often accompanied Mrs. Cameron to the Campbells' cottage when she stayed with Aunt Ellen during holidays.

"Her wee dog's gone missing. I was never a great one for a wee dog myself, though I don't mind a good big animal I'll not be stepping on by accident. I've missed Major, Miss Ellen's golden retriever, since he died."

"Maybe another dog would be good company for us both," Merry put in.

"Aye, well, maybe I could make enquiries,"

offered Mrs. Cameron, "though having to traipse for miles looking for Cailleach last night isn't the best way to get us thinking about a dog again. She's just a wee thing, though . . . a Cairn . . . and she's a right nice wee dog as they go."

"I remember her," said Merry, "only she was just a pup when I saw her last."

"Isa's fair upset, so if you could just keep a look-out for her, Miss Merry, I'd be obliged. Ten to one Jake Grieve's been putting down snares again, and she'll have been caught, poor beast."

"Oh no, I hope not," cried Merry. "He shouldn't be allowed!"

"Maybe no," agreed Mrs. Cameron.

Merry posted her letters quickly, and allowed Maggie Scott to pack her basket neatly for her, and cover it with a layer of tissue and one of brown paper.

"You get wee bits fa'in off the trees at this time o' year," she explained.

"Is your leg better now?" asked Merry politely, referring to a burn Maggie had received while removing a kettle of boiling water off an old-fashioned open grate in one of the cottages.

"Good as new," Maggie told her. "Oh, by the way, Miss Merry, if you've time you could look in on old Mrs. Weir? She needs a form filling in about her old age pension, and she won't have me helping her. It was always Miss Blayne who did that, so I expect she'd prefer you to me."

Merry smiled. She'd learned that part of her duties as new owner of Beau Ness was to witness signatures and help fill in forms for some of the older people.

"I'll do it now," she promised.

It was after three o'clock when she began to make her way back home again, taking a detour through the woods in the hopes of spotting Cailleach. According to Maggie Scott, she still hadn't been found, and poor Isa Campbell "had the face grat off herself".

As Merry swished through the leaves, following the well-trodden path, she felt a little like Red Riding Hood, and smiled at her fancies, though a few moments later she was uneasily aware of being followed. She slowed slightly, hearing the crackle of leaves behind her, and the snap of a twig.

"Who is it?" she called. "Who's there?"

Around her was a great stillness, then a small figure in a well-mended grey jersey and faded jeans slid from behind a tree, and Merry sighed with relief.

"Billy Connell!" she cried. "Are you not at school today?"

"I've had chickenpox," he told her proudly. "It's Matt's turn now, and Mum says Sadie is sickening, too. It goes through the whole lot of us when we pick anything up."

"I see," said Merry, her eyes twinkling as she looked down at the sturdy wee boy with the crew-cut. Joe Connell cut the boys' hair himself and only knew one style.

"What about some chocolate?" she asked, feeling in her basket.

"I could go that," Billy told her appreciatively. "We got some rare soup at dinner time, though, and me dad got some apples up at Rossie House. He's doing odd jobs now for Mr. Kilpatrick."

"That's good," said Merry, not forgetting to look around for the dog.

"What are you casting about for?" asked Billy curiously.

"I'm listening in case we hear Mrs. Campbell's little dog, Cailleach," explained Merry. "She's lost, and I believe the Campbells are upset."

Billy scuffed the leaves.

"No use looking here," he said at length. "The tinkers got her."

Merry came to an abrupt halt.

"The tinkers?" she echoed.

"Aye, they're camping again ower by the loch. I saw the big one carrying a wriggly kind of sack yesterday morning, and I slipped after him. It was the wee dog."

"But what would they want with it?" demanded Merry incredulously.

"Och, they'll bet a couple o' pound for it in Hillington. That wee dog's puir bred."

Merry's eyes widened and her cheeks were

65

beginning to warm with anger. To think of Mrs. Cameron having traipsed for miles, as she'd put it, helping to look for her sister's pet, when the tinkers had it. And the Campbells both heartbroken looking for it.

"And didn't you tell anybody?" she demanded.

Billy shook his head.

"Best lea' tinkers alane, miss," he advised. "They're no like the gypsies. They're just trash and they don't care whether they belt ye on the lug or not. They'd steal the teeth out yer mouth, so they would."

"But we'll have to get the dog back," said Merry. "They can't get away with that!"

"Naebody would go for it," she was informed. "Even the Campbells would be feart. I'll be awa' noo, anyway"

"Show me where they've camped," she said. "I'm going for it."

"You never are, miss!" squealed Billy, and turned to streak for home, until he felt a small firm hand grip his jersey.

"If you're afraid, I'm not," said Merry firmly. "Tinkers or not, they can't go thieving dogs. Show me where the camp is, then you can go home."

"I . . . I can't," said Billy. "Honest, I can't. My dad would skin me alive."

"Would some more chocolate stiffen your nerves?" asked Merry. "Believe me, they won't

66

dare harm you while I'm here. Now, show me the camp, Billy, then you can run home."

"O.K., miss," he said resignedly. "Only don't say I didna warn you."

They crossed the main road and took a path that skirted the loch until it branched off into a wooded section.

"There's a clearing in there, miss," whispered Billy, his eyes large with apprehension. "They've got tents drawn up an' they'll hae a fire lit. I can smell the smoke."

Merry, too, could smell the faint acrid odour of wood smoke.

"Are there many of them, Billy?" she asked.

"No sae mony as the gypsies," he informed her. "The auld man and wumman, an' a hefty young man an' some weans, so likely there's a young wumman tae. The weans are dirty, no like us. That's why my mam gets mad when somebody says we Connells are aboot as bad as the tinkers. We're no like them, are we, miss?"

Merry rumpled his hair above the fresh-skinned young face.

"Never," she whispered. "No one at all is like you, Billy, and don't you forget it."

"Can I go now, miss?" he asked anxiously. "I'll wait for you by the loch side in case you get lost."

Merry nodded, and for a moment faltered in her determination. Something about the atmosphere of the place chilled her, and she felt a pang of unaccustomed fear. Then a faint barking came to her ears, answered by the high-pitched yelping sound of a smaller dog, and she plunged through the trees, her cheeks warming with anger when she remembered the fatigue and concern in Mrs. Cameron's eyes.

She came upon their small settlement suddenly, and stopped to watch the shadowy figures sitting round a crackling fire, their tattered tents forming a background. Three small children sat together, eating silently, while an old witch-like figure picked up a pot from the fire and shook it. Merry could smell the faint aroma of cooking, mingling with the wood smoke. She saw that the children were regarding her with wide-eyed amazement, and a second later the old crone was on her feet.

"Whit'st waant?" she was asked.

Merry slowly walked forward into the clearing, and a dirty-looking old man appeared from behind the tents, a greenish grey muffler tied round his throat. A small barking mongrel appeared with him, baring its teeth, while from behind Merry could hear the faint high yelps of the other dog.

Wetting her lips, she stared the old woman in the eye.

"I've come for the dog," she said clearly.

"Whit dug?"

"Mrs. Campbell's Cairn. I know you've got it."

"Ye ken naethin'. Be off wi' ye!"

68

The old man advanced on her threateningly, and the children came to stand round her. From one of the tents a young woman appeared, and Merry saw that she was heavy with child. She looked across the smoky twilight atmosphere at the girl who was only a few years older than herself, but who looked as though a century stood between them. She pushed back her long dull hair and pulled her jacket closer round her neck.

"I've come for Mrs. Campbell's dog," repeated Merry firmly, looking at the girl with a strangely sick feeling inside. What if she'd been born to this life? she wondered. These people were poor because they refused to accept the responsibilities of society. They were dirty because their living conditions were unhygienic. Yet the gypsies were clean, and kept themselves clean in circumstances little different from the tinkers'.

Merry's stomach turned over a little with distaste, but the dog's frenzied yelps spurred her on, and she took a step forward.

"If you don't give me the dog, I shall go for the police," she told the man.

"Then maybe we should see t'it ye'll not clype tae the polis again."

She whirled at the deep rough voice behind her, and cried aloud as a youngish man caught her arm.

"Let me go!" she said furiously. "How dare you lay a finger on me!"

69

"Ye're trespassin'," he informed her softly. "If I put a foot ower yer doorstep, ye'd be yellin', but ye come here thinkin' tae put a foot ower mine. Wi' lies, tae, my fine lady."

His fingers tightened on her arm and she dropped her basket, twisting in his grasp, her heart thudding with fear.

"They aren't lies," she panted. "I want the dog. You were seen taking it, so I know you've got it. I can even hear it barking!"

"Gie it 'er!" shouted the girl.

"Shut yer mooth," she was told, and Merry's face contorted with pain as the steely fingers gripped her arm.

"Let me go!" she cried again.

"Yes, let her go!"

The fingers dropped from her arm, and she almost stumbled as Benjamin's tall figure emerged from behind her and put his arm round her. She could smell the rough sweetness of his jacket, and leaned against him for a moment.

"What do you think you're doing, you little fool?" his harsh voice demanded of her, and she stepped back as though his tongue had lashed her.

Merry felt her throat tighten with tears, but her chin firmed resolutely.

"They have Isa Campbell's Cairn," she said, firmly. "Mrs. Cameron looked for hours for it yesterday, and Billy Connell saw the old man here stealing it. If they don't hand Cailleach over, I shan't stop till I've brought the police."

Benjamin looked at her small straight figure, a strange look on his face.

"Get it," he told the tinker tersely.

"But, Mr. Benjamin . . ."

"Get it!" repeated Benjamin, and the man shrugged, and made off behind the tents. Merry fixed her eyes on the glowing fire and bubbling pot whose contents were beginning to revolt her. She didn't look at Benjamin because he was giving her a strange desire to burst into tears.

A moment later the tinker returned and threw the whimpering dog at Merry's feet. She bent to pick it up, but Benjamin's warning cry stopped her, and she saw that the little dog's teeth were bared in fright, its eyes wide with terror.

Gently she coaxed it, easing her hand forward, until Cailleach allowed her to stroke her ears, then lift her up into her arms, where the little dog whimpered, then licked her hand. Merry buried her face in the rough coat, and for the first time felt it was all worth while. She was aware of Benjamin guiding her through the trees to the loch-side path, and of young Billy running to meet them.

"So you found her, sir!" he cried. "I'm real glad!"

"And you'd no business to leave her there," said Benjamin, though the hard steely note had left his voice. "Home with you, young Billy. I might be along to skelp you in the morning."

"Yes, sir," said the boy.

"As for you, Merry Saunders, I shan't start to you tonight, but I'm astonished you showed so little sense. Have you never been told to leave the tinkers alone? I never thought a young woman could be such a fool! No wonder Ellen thought you needed an eye kept on you."

"I suppose Stephanie would have had more sense," said Merry angrily.

"Whatever we may think of Stephanie," Benjamin told her quietly, "no one could ever doubt her ability to look after herself. She never causes anxiety on that account. Here's Beau Ness. I'll see Mrs. Cameron gets you up to bed."

"But Cailleach ought to go home," protested Merry tearfully. "The Campbells will want her. Besides, it isn't late."

"Don't worry, young Bill will have spread the gospel. Isa will be here before you can say knife. She'll take no hurt with a good meal inside her, and a rest in front of the fire."

As they walked through the door, and Mrs. Cameron listened incredulously to Benjamin's explanations, Merry felt she could have dropped with fatigue. Then she remembered the basket.

"It's still there . . . at the tinkers'," she cried.

"Mercy, my good basket!" cried Mrs. Cameron. "Oh, Miss Merry!"

"I'll get it back tomorrow," said Merry, and

again Benjamin looked her with the odd gleam in his eye.

"I wouldna want it," declared Mrs. Cameron, firmly, "wi' that crowd pawing their dirt all over it. I wouldna touch it wi' a barge pole, Miss Merry, and your Aunt Ellen's best basket she bought years ago. Ye can't get the likes these days."

"Then they'll have been paid well for the dog!" put in Benjamin, preparing to go.

"Maybe those ... those little children will get something decent to eat out of it, p—poor th—things," said Merry, and burst into tears.

"Poor little kid," said Benjamin, his voice suddenly inexpressibly tender. "Put her to bed, Mrs. Cameron, do. She's had a frightening experience."

Sobbing, and ashamed that Benjamin should see her tears, Merry allowed Mrs. Cameron to lead her off to bed.

The post was late, and Merry was already at her desk when Mrs. Cameron brought in a few letters and a bulky envelope. Merry took one look at it and felt her heart sink.

"Oh, no!" she sighed, disappointed. "It's my short story back. It's bounced like a rubber ball."

She eyed the rejection slip which gave no clue as to the reason for its return, and ran her fingers through her hair, then began to re-read the manuscript carefully. If she still thought it good enough, then it would be offered to another market straight away.

"Mr. Benjamin's here, Miss Merry," said Mrs. Cameron, as she brought in a cup of coffee. "Will I tell him you're busy?"

"No, no, of course not. It's good of him to come. Ask him to come through, Mrs. Cameron."

"I'll hand him in a cup of coffee, too," beamed Mrs. Cameron, and a moment later Benjamin walked into the study.

"Busy?" he asked. "I only popped over to see how you were. I believe Mrs. Campbell's singing your praises all over Kilbraggan."

Merry blushed.

"I wish she wouldn't," she said ruefully. "She was so delighted to have Cailleach back."

She laid aside the manuscript with a sigh.

"I'm not doing too well at the moment," she told him despondently. "I was sure this would sell, but I see now that it's away off the mark. I wrote it rather emotionally, and the characters are quite unbelievable. I'll have to scrap it."

Benjamin leafed it over.

"I know how you feel," he told her sympathetically. "I used to have some of my work rejected, and it knocked the stuffing out of me for an hour or two. What about the book?"

"I've made a start," Merry told him. "I only wanted to keep on with a few articles and short stories in the meantime. Nigel's coming over to help me with an article on cleaning jewellery, this afternoon."

Benjamin pursed his lips, and nodded.

"Best let you get on with it, then," he told her, easing himself off her desk.

"Och, but I've just made you some coffee, Mr. Benjamin," said Mrs. Cameron, appearing with a tray, and Benjamin relaxed again, as he thanked her and began to drink his coffee.

"You . . . you seem to get on well with Nigel Kilpatrick," he said casually, as he helped himself to a buttered scone.

Merry nodded.

"He's been very nice to me."

"You . . . er . . . like him?"

She looked at him defensively.

"Of course I do. He's charming. As a matter of fact, I've promised to help again at their next jewellery display in the Royal Hotel at Hillington. Will you be going?"

Benjamin put down his cup and stood up.

"I think I opt out this time," he told her. "That sort of glamour isn't really my line, and you already know what I think of you becoming involved with their jewellery. I know nothing went wrong last time, but that doesn't mean that I think the possibility no longer exists. Anyway, if you must do this sort of thing, I can't stop you . . . only don't get into more scrapes, will you? I might not always be available to bail you out!"

"I told you I didn't want a watch-dog," she said with a touch of annoyance.

He nodded and turned to go.

"Cheerio, Merry."

"Cheerio," she returned, and watched him go, feeling a sudden attack of unaccustomed loneliness. Benjamin had said he might not always be available, and the thought depressed her, while she wondered exactly what he had meant. Surely he wasn't leaving the Cot House? Or could it be that he would be devoting more time to Stephanie in the future? Merry found the thought oddly depressing, though she didn't know just why this could be so.

With a sigh, she picked up her manuscript and tore it across, dropping it in her wastepaper basket. It was an emotional story, and that was the place for emotions which didn't do any good.

Nigel arrived after lunch, and Merry greeted him brightly, if a little subdued.

"Hello, Nigel, it's so nice to see you. Oh, you've brought me some notes, thank goodness. I need them. I got my last short story back today."

"Too bad," said Nigel, and Merry's eyes flickered as she realised it didn't really mean anything to him. "I hope you'll make a better job of your article, then."

He began sorting out the papers.

"I've made a heading for each type of stone,

and a note under it as to how best to keep it clean. Diamonds, as you see here, can actually be boiled clean, dried in hot sawdust, then polished gently with a soft cloth. Some people are terrified of washing them in case the stone comes out of the setting, which is nonsense. They're probably confusing the diamonds with a much softer stone like turquoise. Anyway, a well-set stone won't come out with soap and water, and you'd be surprised how dirty jewellery can get."

"It's bound to, when you think about it," said Merry.

She watched Nigel's eyes light up when he warmed to his subject, and had to admit that he was very attractive, as his bright blue eyes smiled into hers.

"I remember a woman buying a spinel eternity ring, when I was working as an assistant in one of the shops. White spinels look a little like diamonds at first glance, though there's less fire and a more whiteish appearance. At any rate, the spinels were much cheaper, and she chose the ring after being assured that they were genuine gemstones. A few weeks later she was back, declaring she'd been had, and the ring was nothing but cheap glass. The stones were dull and lifeless, and the ring looked terrible. It took me about five minutes to clean it up in our workroom, then she was suspicious that I'd swapped it over for another ring! You can't please everybody."

He leafed over a page.

"Be careful what you say about pearls, though, in case someone goes off and boils them! They need a great deal more care, and must be cleaned with warm soapy water to get the grease off, then dried very gently. Turquoises, too, are soft and have to be cleaned very carefully. The blue can lose its colour in water, warm water that is, so don't do the washing up wearing a turquoise ring. I can give you some good illustrations if it will help your article."

"Oh, Nigel, you are good," cried Merry, and he turned to her with a smile.

"Am I, Merry?"

He reached out and drew her gently into his arms, kissing her. She tried to respond, feeling the need to have someone to care for her, someone she could love in return. She could easily love Nigel, she decided, even if she didn't think she was in love with him.

"What's wrong, Merry?" he asked, pushing her hair back and looking into her face. "I thought you were beginning to care for me. You know, I love you quite a lot already, but I was going to give you more time for us to get to know each other. I know you're not a girl to be rushed."

"No," said Merry, shaking her head, "and I do like you, Nigel."

"Then can't I kiss you properly?"

"I . . . I think I'm a little tired today," she excused herself.

"Our consorting with the tinkers?" asked Nigel teasingly, though there was a warning note in his voice. "Not the sort of escapade I enjoy my girl getting up to."

"Who told you?" asked Merry.

"Oh, darling, everything that happens in Kilbraggan is news in five minutes. I expect we're even engaged by now, in some quarters, though we haven't got as far as that yet . . . have we?"

She shook her head.

"Not yet, Nigel. As you say, I don't like being rushed. We both need more time."

"But not too much," said Nigel softly, and kissed her again.

Outside Merry could hear the faint sound of a car, growing louder as it turned into the drive and crunched on the gravel.

"Who can that be?" she asked. "Stephanie come to take you home?"

"I've got my own car," he told her, "and it sounds more like Joe Weir."

A moment later the bell shrilled, and Mrs. Cameron padded to the front door.

"I'd better be going, Merry. What about a run out in the car next Saturday? We could drive somewhere for dinner . . . maybe dancing, too."

"That would be lovely," said Merry, feeling her spirits lift. Nigel was really very sweet. The faint sounds of a female voice reached her, and she turned as Mrs. Cameron again knocked gently on the door.

"Ye've got a visitor, Miss Merry," she announced, a rather constrained note in her voice. "It's yer cousin, Miss Neilson."

"Sylvia!" cried Merry. "Whatever is she doing here?" and a moment later an all-too-familiar voice was greeting her.

"Merry darling, I knew you'd want me to come, though I've had such a journey from the station with that peculiar old taxi driver, Joe Something ... Oh!"

She stopped in the doorway, looking like a silver fairy with her pale dove-grey suit, matching accessories and wonderful silvery-blonde hair. Her small piquant face was flushed, her eyes sparkling with a mixture of annoyance and excitement, and Merry had never seen her look lovelier. Even Stephanie's beauty paled into more ordinary good looks beside Sylvia.

"This is Mr. Kilpatrick, from Rossie House," she said, turning to Nigel. "Nigel, my cousin, Sylvia Neilson."

"How do you do."

Sylvia's voice tinkled sweetly and her small face dimpled into a smile as she held out her hand. Merry had seen that look so many times before, and the smile went a bit stiff on her face. Would Nigel, too, be captivated, even at first sight, as so many before had been?

"I was just going, I'm afraid," he said, politely but rather formally, "but I shall be back over to see Merry shortly. We'll meet again, Miss Neilson."

"I'll look forward to that," Sylvia told him, laughter gleaming in her eyes.

Merry accompanied him to the door, and he turned to wave cheerfully and tell her that he'd see her soon. She returned to the sitting-room, to find Sylvia sprawling on the settee, her luggage piled round her. She didn't know whether she was glad to see her cousin or not.

"Well, Sylvia?" asked Merry.

"I'd forgotten how restful it is, darling," said Sylvia, waving her hand about, "so quiet. Just what I need at the moment. I hope you'll be very sweet and won't mind if I stay for a week or two."

Merry felt mean and ashamed that her heart sank at Sylvia's words. She ought to be happy to have her only cousin here to stay, but she had never grown very fond of Sylvia, and the thought of having to put up with her for more than a very short visit depressed her.

"If you won't be bored," she said flatly. "What about Graham? Won't he be missing you?"

"Not much," said Sylvia, rather airily.

"That's all over, and don't get stuffy and start asking questions. We were never really suited, you know."

Merry's lips tightened. She'd liked Graham Holland, and Sylvia had only wanted him because he was her friend. Luckily her heart hadn't been touched, but she suspected that Graham had been hurt, and was annoyed that Sylvia could treat people so casually.

"How are Aunt Elizabeth and Uncle George?" she asked, changing the subject.

"A bit peevish with you, Merry dear, for running out on them."

Her voice changed suddenly, and she looked very young and tired with faint blue shadows under her eyes.

"They drive me to screaming point at times," she said, "and it's worse since you left. Let me stay here for a while, anyway. I feel tired to death, and I want a change. I want peace and quiet, for once."

Merry's heart softened. If only Sylvia would shed all her affectations permanently, and try to live a normal, useful life, how much easier it would be to love her. They were cousins, and they should be much closer than they were. She had been spoilt by Aunt Elizabeth and Uncle George doting on her, but it wasn't too late for her to learn new values.

"Of course you can stay, Sylvia, as I told

you," she said warmly. "I'll be glad to have you. It gets a little bit lonely at times."

"With such an attractive young man?" asked Sylvia teasingly, and laughed as Merry blushed. "Tell me about him. Who is he, and what does he do?"

Merry began to tell her all about the Kilpatrick shops, pleased to be arousing Sylvia's interest as she told her all about the jewellery exhibition.

"And you mean you modelled that fabulous jewellery?" asked Sylvia incredulously. "Wow! You have been having a lovely time. Lucky Stephanie. She'll be able to borrow what she wants."

"Perhaps," smiled Merry. "Though I think they consider the stock is for selling to their customers, and not for private use."

"I hope I can have a peep. I love jewellery and precious stones. Those brooches and things old Aunt Julia left me are so old-fashioned now. I'd love to see those cocktail rings, and brooches, modern-designed brooches. Could I see them, do you think?"

Merry laughed at the eagerness on her cousin's young face. In this mood, Sylvia was irresistible.

"I expect so, darling."

A moment later Mrs. Cameron walked in, a guarded look on her normally cheerful face.

"I've put Miss Neilson in your old room, Miss

Merry," she said, a trifle stiffly. "I hope that's all right."

"That will be wonderful, Mrs. Cameron," cried Sylvia. "And please call me Sylvia. Surely you remember me when I used to come and stay with Aunt Ellen. Merry and I were often here together."

"I remember you, Miss . . . Sylvia," Mrs. Cameron informed her, in the same disapproving voice.

"And no doubt thought me a horrible child," laughed Sylvia disarmingly. "Oh, Mrs. Cameron, don't hold it against me. Look! I've grown up now."

She rose, turning and twisting for the older woman's inspection, and Mrs. Cameron's expression reluctantly softened into a smile. Sylvia could be lively and full of fun when she liked, thought Merry. It might be nice to have another girl around for a little while.

"You can have a warm bath before your supper, Miss Sylvia," Mrs. Cameron told her, as she hurried towards the kitchen. "I'll take the rest of your things up to the bedroom."

"Thank you," said Sylvia. "I'll just go up now, then, Merry. This is going to be fun!"

CHAPTER 5

IT was difficult to settle into a new routine, thought Merry, as she struggled with the third chapter of her book, even with the encouragement of an acceptance for her jewellery article. Sylvia was doing her best to fit into the household, although Mrs. Cameron was alternately disapproving and resigned. She deplored the untidiness in Sylvia's bedroom, then softened a little when the girl brought her some small gift from the village stores, or Hillington.

At first she had found it difficult to understand why Merry was willing to do anything so boring as writing. It was much too reminiscent of school essays and tiresome homework, but Merry knew that explanations were almost impossible, and merely made it clear that her study was her own domain, and privacy was essential.

The following Saturday Merry got ready for her date with Nigel, while Sylvia watched her, the first look of sulkiness on her face.

"I do think you might ask Nigel to take me, too," she said, pouting. "It's bad manners going out and leaving me here on my own."

Merry forbore to point out the number of times she had been left on her own, while Sylvia went dancing, and her aunt and uncle attended a bridge party.

"You'll have Mrs. Cameron," she pointed out. "You won't be entirely on your own."

"What fun!" exclaimed Sylvia sarcastically.

"I'm sorry you feel that way," said Merry. "I'm afraid Nigel asked me before we knew you were coming, Sylvia."

"Well, you've no right to leave me here bored to death," Sylvia retorted sulkily, then brightened a little. "Maybe Nigel will ask me to come, too, when he calls."

"Maybe he will," said Merry quietly. "I shan't need to give you any advice on how to wangle an invitation."

Nigel looked tall and handsome in a dark suit and sparkling white shirt, and Merry felt a rush of pride at the sight of him. Sylvia had beaten Mrs. Cameron to the door, and was now sweetly entertaining him, and offering him cigarettes. Nigel's blue eyes sparkled with amusement at her eager efforts to amuse him.

"I do think Merry's lucky, going out dancing," she told him. "I love dancing."

"Most young people do," Nigel told her smilingly. "I tell you what . . ." He paused, and Sylvia gazed at him eagerly.

"Yes?"

"My sister Stephanie is in London at the moment, on business for our firm. We're running another line in gold jewellery, which has been enamelled in glowing colours, and we thought Stephanie might take a look at the latest samples. The one sent to us was a lovely brooch, shaped like a flower, and enamelled in rich blues

86

and greens, with diamonds on the stem. It isn't a new idea, of course, but fairly new to Kilpatricks."

Sylvia's eyes were glowing.

"How gorgeous!" she breathed. "I'd love to see them."

"And so you shall," said Nigel indulgently. "Stephanie will be buying a few pieces, brooches, rings and bracelets, and we'll see if they become popular or not. When she comes home, I'm sure she'll be delighted to arrange a small party. Brendan would come, and one or two young people from Hillington. We'll make sure of the dancing, Sylvia."

"Who is Brendan?" she asked.

"Benjamin Brendan who lives in the Cot House. He's a commercial artist. Hasn't Merry mentioned him?"

"There hasn't been much time to tell Sylvia about everyone yet," Merry said, rather hastily, her cheeks suddenly warm. It was difficult to know why she had put off introducing Sylvia to Benjamin.

"Talk of the devil," said Nigel, as he glanced out of the window, "here he is now."

Benjamin looked amused when he saw the small party in the sitting-room.

"Well, well," he said, walking forward. "Have I come at the wrong time? All set for a night out?"

"Except me," Sylvia told him, in a small voice, while Merry quickly made the introductions.

"Don't let me keep you," Benjamin told her. "I only came over with the rest of the information about Uncle Ian for your book. I thought you might be waiting for it."

"Oh, Benjamin, I am," said Merry delightedly. "I'll be able to get on with it so much quicker. Thank you very much."

She was aware of three pairs of eyes regarding her, but Nigel and Sylvia were only curious, while Benjamin was understanding.

"We'd best not waste much more time, Merry," said Nigel, a trifle impatiently.

"Sorry I've called at the wrong time," said Benjamin again, and Sylvia regarded him with an impish smile.

"Oh, please don't go just yet," she pleaded. "Couldn't you stay a little while and talk to me? I was going to be left on my own while Merry went out enjoying herself."

"Now, it wasn't like that at all," cried Merry, colouring.

"Wasn't it?" Sylvia's enormous eyes opened wide. "Were you going to take me, too?"

"Come on, Merry," said Nigel crossly. "I'm sure Sylvia and Benjamin can make each other's acquaintance very well on their own."

Merry bit her lip, very much aware of Benjamin's quizzical stare. It was unfair of Sylvia to give the impression that she was selfish and lacking in consideration. She felt strangely ruffled inside at the sight of Sylvia smiling charmingly at Benjamin, and had to remind herself again that Benjamin's private life had nothing to do with her. He only looked on her as a child, and a responsibility. Besides, it was Stephanie who would have to watch out for Sylvia, and she was well able to take care of herself.

"Cheerio, then," she said awkwardly, picking up her bag, and allowing Nigel to slip a wrap round her shoulders.

"Have a good time," said Sylvia sweetly, looking like a kitten faced with a dish of cream. "No need to be early."

"We won't be late," said Merry shortly.

She allowed Nigel to settle her in the car, feeling as though her feathers had been ruffled, and all her enjoyment of the evening spoilt, and it annoyed her that she should feel this way.

"I thought we'd go to the Blue Cockerel," said Nigel, as he guided the car out of the drive. "It's just a new place, and doing very well, I hear, and they've a small band for dancing. How about it, Merry?"

"Fine, thanks, Nigel," she agreed.

It should have been delightful, she thought later, as she danced in Nigel's arms. It was everything she had ever dreamed, but the carefree happiness she should have enjoyed was lacking, and Merry felt confused. She could only see Benjamin's inscrutable face with his slight smile, as he waved them goodbye, then turn to smile down at Sylvia.

It was quite late when they arrived back at Beau Ness, and Merry asked Nigel in for a quick hot drink before he went home.

"It will help you to sleep," she smiled, as she boiled up milk.

"I shall have pleasant dreams, too," teased Nigel, and turned her round to kiss her. "It's been a lovely evening. Let's do it again some time."

Merry's heart lifted. Nigel hadn't even mentioned Sylvia. At least he hadn't lost his heart in double quick time to her lovely cousin. He was loyal to her, and was showing no inclination to drop her, as soon as Sylvia came on the scene, as had happened so often before.

"I'd love that, Nigel," she said, with a sudden rush of affection.

"I'll come over one evening during the week after Stephanie comes home, and we can take Sylvia to Rossie House, and let her see some of the new pieces. I can bring some other stuff home from the shop, too."

"She'd love that, I'm sure. Goodnight, Nigel."

"Goodnight, darling."

He kissed her gently, and she closed the door

as quietly as she could, then turned as a ghostly figure glided down the stairs.

"For heaven's sake, Sylvia, haven't you got a warmer dressing-gown than that piece of lace?" Merry asked crossly.

"It isn't cold," said Sylvia. "And, anyway, I want a hot drink, too. Was it nice?"

"Very."

"Your other boy-friend didn't stay long. He's quite sweet, really, though not nearly so nice as Nigel."

"He's not my other boy-friend," said Merry, sharply. "As a matter of fact, he and Stephanie are friends."

"Ah, I see," said Sylvia thoughtfully. "She'll be lucky if she gets him. He looks like one of those self-sufficient types, if you ask me."

Merry didn't want to discuss Benjamin, or Nigel, with her cousin.

"Sorry, Sylvia," she said, "I'm awfully tired. I'll see you at breakfast."

"O.K.," said Sylvia lightly, and watched Merry walk upstairs. She had changed a lot, thought Sylvia, and wondered if Merry realised it. She'd always been inclined to be a bit of a mouse, but now she had a new authority about her. Merry was someone to be reckoned with now, and if Sylvia wanted anything which didn't meet with her approval, she'd have a fight on her hands.

There was an air of excitement about her, as

she, too, climbed the stairs, and she had never looked lovelier. Having to fight for what she wanted might be . . . quite a lot of fun!

Despite disruptions in the house, Merry's book began to make progress, though she knew it was essential not to spend too much time at her desk, but to try to go for a walk when she could.

She had not seen Benjamin since the night she went out with Nigel, and a sudden longing to talk to him again assailed her. Sylvia had gone to Hillington for the day, deciding that she needed some clothes, and Merry felt light and free as she took the winding road to the Cot House.

"I shall go away, if you're busy," she told Benjamin, when he opened the door. "I've an errand in the village, in any case, for Mrs. Cameron."

"I'm fairly busy," Benjamin admitted honestly, "but don't go running away. It's seldom the Cot House is honoured."

Merry had got used to Benjamin's turn of phrase now, and only nodded as she made her way to the settee in front of the fire. His working section of the room was littered with open books and papers, and she saw he was busy on a line and wash drawing at his board.

"My weekly comic strip," he told her. "Nearly finished, though. How's the book?"

"Progressing," she assured him. "I can't judge it, though. It may be pretty poor stuff."

"Are you any good on children's stories?" asked Benjamin, as he switched on the kettle, and lifted down two beakers. Merry enjoyed his strong brew, and knew better than to offer to help.

"What sort of stories?" she asked.

"Oh, books for the little ones. I've wondered sometimes if it wouldn't be fun to do one, only I couldn't write the story. They aren't easy, though people don't always realise that. How about it, Merry?"

"You mean collaborate on a children's story book?" she asked, her eyes beginning to sparkle. "I could do the story, and you could illustrate it." She paused thoughtfully. "That would be a lot of fun. But . . ."

"Fifty-fifty," said Benjamin promptly.

"I happen to know that wouldn't be fair," said Merry knowledgeably. "The illustrations sell that sort of story. They're most important."

"Let's see how we go," suggested Benjamin. "Shall we try it?"

"Done," she agreed, and held out her hand, feeling her heart lurch as he grasped it in his strong, lean fingers. For a moment he caressed her fingers, then dropped her hand and filled up the beakers with tea.

"Is your cousin still here?"

Merry nodded. "She likes it, strange as it may

seem. Sylvia has usually been a town girl, and loves a busy social life, but she's finding Kilbraggan far from quiet. She might even stay for Christmas, and if so, Aunt Elizabeth and Uncle George may come, too. I used to live with them, you know."

"But you like it better on your own?" asked Benjamin, and Merry nodded.

"Does it sound selfish of me? I loved having the house to myself, and being by myself whenever I wanted. I can't think or work with people around, and my work is becoming important to me."

"More important than marriage when the time comes?" asked Benjamin.

She hesitated, her face thoughtful, before replying:

"No . . . No, I don't think so. It would depend on how much I loved . . . someone . . . If I cared about a man, he would come first."

"Lucky chap," said Benjamin, "and adult views from a young girl." His voice became teasing. "Anyone special in mind?"

"I'll have to wait till I'm asked," she said laughingly, matching his light mood. "Anyway, I shall leave you to your work. Thank you for the tea. Shall I let you have some small stories soon?"

"Please," agreed Benjamin. "Five- to eight-year-olds would be best."

Merry's step was light as she left the Cot

House and walked towards Isa Campbell's cottage, with a message from Mrs. Cameron.

"Come awa' ben, Miss Merry," the woman greeted her, as she knocked on the door. "I'm fair pleased to see you. Get down, Cailleach!"

The little dog was jumping round Merry excitedly, and she bent to stroke the shaggy coat while the soft dark eyes regarded her eagerly.

"Is she none the worse, Mrs. Campbell?"

"None the worse, thank goodness," Isa told her. "Thanks to you. Thon tinkers are awa' noo, Miss Merry, and good riddance. If it hadn't been for you, dear knows where my wee dog would have been."

Merry sat down on a comfortable old chair by the fire, and delivered Mrs. Cameron's message to her sister.

"Bessie is going to help with the Church Bazaar at Christmas, then," she said. "That's good. Her ginger cake and shortbread aye go well. I like Christmas. It fair brightens the place up after autumn. We could sometimes do wi' a few more social events, though I believe there's a dance or two organised, and we might see a bit of excitement when Miss Kilpatrick gets married."

Merry blinked a little with surprise.

"Married?" she asked.

"Och, my tongue runs away wi' me at times." said Isa Campbell, confused. "We're no supposed to ken anything aboot it. It's just that I've a cousin, Jeanie Lumsden, works for them, and Miss Stephanie aye gives her her old magazines to bring to me. She had a nice posh fashion one, and all the wedding dresses were marked with pencil, so it looks like something's in the wind, doesn't it?"

"It does," agreed Merry in a small voice.

Why hadn't Benjamin told her, she wondered, instead of making plans for collaborating with her over a child's book? Knowing Stephanie, she wouldn't relish such co-operation between her new husband and another girl, however innocent it would be.

Merry rose, accepting a small basket of eggs that Mrs. Campbell had ready for her sister.

"I'd better make tracks for home," she said, with a small smile. "It gets dark so early at the moment. Cheerio, Mrs. Campbell."

"Daunder doon again, Miss Merry," the older woman told her. "We don't see enough of you these days, and we fair miss Miss Ellen. One or twa folk were asking if ye'd gie them a wee keek in."

"I'll make a point of coming later in the week," promised Merry.

But her thoughts were all for Benjamin, as she walked home in the gloaming. She was nearing the turn off along the loch-side, and nostalgia gripped her as she remembered clinging, frightened, to the rough tweed of Benjamin's jacket, and breathing in the clean sweetness of him as he held her close. He'd been angry, but deep down she knew that his rage had been based on fear for her.

Now, with almost unbearable longing, she wanted to feel his arms round her again. There would be such peace and security in her heart, if only ... if only ...

Merry forced back the tears, as she realised what these feelings for Benjamin meant. She loved him with all her heart. He was the one man for whom she would be willing to give up everything, even her very life. Yet he belonged to another girl, and Merry scrubbed her eyes vigorously at the thought. If Stephanie hadn't really loved him, Merry would have felt differently about that, but she was sure Stephanie did love him, and would want to make him happy.

"I only want him to be happy," she told herself, aloud, as she turned in the drive of Beau Ness. "Just so long as Benjamin is happy ..."

Merry had barely taken her coat off and delivered the eggs to Mrs. Cameron, together with all the news which Mrs. Campbell had asked her to pass on, when car wheels crunched in the drive.

"That's Joe Weir's auld taxi again," said Mrs. Cameron. "I ken it a mile awa'."

A moment later a radiantly happy Sylvia

danced in, a large number of packages in her arms.

"What a marvellous day I've had!" she cried, dropping her parcels on to the settee. "I've got the most gorgeous little suit, and a heavenly dress which will be perfect for the jewellery cocktail party. Nigel said I could come to that. Oh, and here's a scarf for you, Merry, and something for Mrs. Cameron."

"Och, you shouldn't spend your money on me, Miss Sylvia," protested Mrs. Cameron, opening her small parcel to find a neat little bottle of perfume. "Oh, isn't it bonny?" she exclaimed, sniffing and trying it out on her blouse. "Just like flowers. Thank you very much, Miss Sylvia."

"Are they early Christmas gifts or something?" laughed Merry, trying on her gay woollen scarf.

"Just wait till I try on my dress and suit," Sylvia told her, disappearing upstairs, while Mrs. Cameron shook her head and Merry turned her eyes up to the ceiling. Their visit to Rossie House had been postponed until Saturday as the Kilpatrick were very busy with a pre-Christmas rush, and Sylvia was full of impatience.

"Tea's going to be late this day," Mrs. Cameron forecast. "We'll never get that lass at the table under half an hour!"

The dress and suit were beautiful, and Merry examined both of them critically, then admiringly.

"They're lovely, Sylvia," she told her cousin. "Where did you get them?"

"Well . . ." For the first time a rather guarded look came over Sylvia's face. "Well, as a matter of fact, I went to that little boutique where you told me you bought your things . . . Estelle's."

"Estelle's?" cried Merry. "Then you couldn't have done better, though they are a bit pricey. I can't go trotting there every day."

Sylvia carefully hung away the suit.

"Well, I hope you don't mind, darling," she said airily, "that I just put these two small things on your account. I'm awfully hard up at the moment, and I do need them. I mean, you won't want me to be shabby when we go out with your friends, will you?"

Merry was speechless for a moment, then her body began to shake with anger. Sylvia had a large dress allowance from her father, and her wardrobe had always been stuffed with clothes. She'd always had to be careful, and only managed to dress well by choosing her clothes intelligently. She'd been hoping to buy a new cocktail dress herself, and had reluctantly decided it would have to wait, and now Sylvia had used her account to buy her own clothes!

"How dare you!" she burst out at length. "You . . . with all your clothing allowance . . . making use of my account!"

"Well, darling," said Sylvia sweetly, "I'm

afraid Daddy and I have had a slight misunderstanding over my clothing allowance, and that's why I decided to come and stay here for a short while, because he was just a little bit angry. Mummy quite understood, but he wouldn't listen to us, so it's quite true I'm hard up. And after all, darling, you got all this gorgeous house, and lots of other things besides, from Aunt Ellen, while I got nothing at all. I thought it was rather unfair, didn't you?"

"But you didn't mind inheriting from Aunt Julie," retorted Merry, her eyes sparkling, "and you were pretty scathing about Beau Ness any time we came to stay. I seem to remember that it was a backwater, and you wouldn't be seen dead in it."

"My mature taste hadn't developed," explained Sylvia. "I like it much better now."

"Perhaps you would also like to share the cost of the upkeep," suggested Merry. "No, my dear, you can jolly well pay for your own clothes, or take them back."

"You're tired, Merry," said Sylvia placatingly. "We'll talk about it another time, shall we?" Carefully she folded away her new purchases "Now, what's for tea? I'm starving!"

On Saturday evening Nigel came over to collect Merry and Sylvia, and take them back to Rossie House. Stephanie had arranged a small party, and one or two young people from Kilpatricks were also there. Mr. Kilpatrick was not present because he had flown over to Ireland on business.

Sylvia wore her new suit, and looked breathtakingly beautiful. Merry saw Nigel blink, then reluctant admiration fill his eyes when he saw her, but it did not hurt as it might have done. She knew now that she had never been really in love with Nigel, nor, she was sure, did he truly love her. They had been greatly attracted to each other, but it had been a lukewarm affair compared to the deep, passionate, lasting love which she was beginning to feel for Benjamin. She was going to need all her courage and determination to control her feelings for him, knowing he could never care for her in return.

Merry sighed. She was again wearing her russet suit which looked charming, but which Rossie House was beginning to know very well, and for a brief moment she allowed herself a pang of anger and resentment against Sylvia. She had received her statement of account from Estelle's and had gasped when she saw what she had to pay, going in search of Sylvia.

"I think it's about time I told you exactly how our finances at Beau Ness are managed," she said crisply, "and how much money Aunt Ellen left to cover all expenses."

Sylvia had replied airily when Merry gave her a few facts and figures, though there had been an air of bravado about her which made

Merry think that some of the lesson had gone home. She would try to meet this bill, she decided, but she must prevent a repetition of the same thing.

"What about all that scribbling?" asked Sylvia scornfully. "I thought it had you rolling in no time."

"Then you can think again," returned Merry. "I'm lucky if I sell two or three articles a month, and short stories are more difficult than ever. My book is making good progress, but I can't even be sure of selling that when it's finished."

"Then why bother?"

Merry drew a deep breath, and wondered, herself, why she bothered.

"Because I must," she said quietly. "I don't expect you to understand, Sylvia, but it's just something I have to do."

Sylvia shrugged and yawned. "Rather you than me, darling," she said.

Merry had managed to write several short stories for children, however, after doing a bit of research into what modern children like, or what modern publishers think modern children ought to like. The results had pleased and excited her, and she ran quickly down the road to the Cot House to deliver them to Benjamin. He was busy, and treated her rather abstractedly, but she knew better than to worry about his offhand manner.

"Put them down on the table, Merry," he

said, intent on his board. "I'll look at them later. Leave me to think about them for a few days."

"O.K., Benjamin," she told him. "Cheerio."

Now she wondered if she would see him tonight, as she had a quick word with Mrs. Cameron over how late they were likely to be, and followed Nigel and Sylvia out to the car.

Sylvia exclaimed with pleasure when she saw Rossie House. Stephanie came forward to meet them, and offer them drinks, while one or two young men and girls were introduced, rather shyly.

Merry found herself shaking hands with the young giant of a man with crisp dark curling hair and snapping black eyes whom she had seen at the first cocktail party. She learned that he was David Bruce, the Hillington shop manager, and was quite an authority on valuing precious stones. He was an F.G.A. and had also made a study of antique silver.

Stephanie was looking very smart in a soft silvery blue dress, her lovely hair immaculately dressed. She hadn't Sylvia's breathtaking beauty, but she ran her a very close second. Merry saw the two girls eye each other warily, then shake hands as Nigel introduced them. She felt that they'd probably have weighed each other up to a 'T'. They would take their time on deciding whether or not they'd be friends.

Then Stephanie was coming forward for a word with her, and Merry again felt herself withdrawing inwardly. She respected Stephanie, knowing that the other girl undertook to do a responsible job for the firm, but deep down they would never really be comfortable with one another.

"Hello, Merry," the other girl greeted her. "So you've acquired an addition to the family."

"Sylvia is only staying temporarily," Merry told her. "She's used to a busier life than Kilbraggan."

"Seems like she's getting it," said Stephanie dryly, her eyes suddenly glittering as they turned to watch Sylvia flirt charmingly with David Bruce. There was an odd expression on Stephanie's face, then she smiled slowly with amusement.

"Benjamin's late," she remarked, then walked forward as his tall figure appeared in the doorway. "Oh, here he is now. Excuse me."

Merry watched while Stephanie hurried over to greet Benjamin, talking to him animatedly, then bringing him over to perform the introductions. Nigel was standing silently at Merry's elbow, after seeing that she had everything she wanted, but she saw that his gaze was now all for Sylvia.

"She's very . . . lovely," he said. "Sylvia, I mean. Has . . . has she had many boy-friends?"

"Quite a few," admitted Merry honestly. "Maybe the right one will settle her down."

"It's difficult to settle a flame," he remarked.

"Much better to keep it burning than to quench it, when it throws such a bright light. Oh, Merry . . . sorry, my dear, would you care for another drink? I hope you don't think I'm neglecting you."

She laughed happily.

"Don't worry about me, Nigel. I'm used to looking after myself, and I quite like it. You can go after the flame, if you wish, only try not to get burned, my dear. I don't like to see my friends hurt."

Nigel looked at her searchingly.

"Then we are friends?" he asked softly. "I'm a fool, Merry. Your warmth is worth ninety flames, but . . ."

"But it doesn't blaze strongly enough for real love," she said softly. "We're good friends, and always will be, but we haven't hurt each other."

"Bless you," he said huskily. "Would you know what I mean if I said I still love you, Merry?"

She nodded.

"Of course. That goes for me, too."

He slipped away and she jumped, startled, as Benjamin appeared behind her. How long had he been there? she wondered, then decided that it didn't really matter.

"You made me jump!" she accused him.

"Sorry, my dear, but you ought to choose moonlight and scented gardens for making sentimental speeches, not small gatherings like this one."

She flushed. So he had heard, even if it was just a small part of it.

"Surely that's our business, Nigel's and mine," she told him, a touch of the old asperity in her tone.

"Of course, of course. I suppose you're in no mood to talk business."

"What business?"

"The little Pink Caterpillar," he said. "I liked it. How do you think he looks?"

He drew a rough illustration out of his pocket, and Merry gasped when she saw one of the characters of her imagination smiling at her from the piece of paper. He had a funny, lopsided grin and huge innocent eyes with long eyelashes.

"Oh, he's sweet!" she exclaimed with delight. "He's really adorable!"

"I shall do one or two proper illustrations, and send them up to my agent, with a mock-up of the book. I like this one. In a funny way it reminds me of you."

"Why?" asked Merry, wrinkling her brows as she strove to recall her little pink caterpillar who carried on courageously through life in spite of a great many adversities.

"Oh, I don't know . . . just somehow . . . until this evening, that is."

She regarded him for a moment, still puzzled.

"The little pink caterpillar fought for what he wanted in his own quiet way," said Benjamin quietly.

"Don't you think that was wise of him?"

"Very wise. By the way, your cousin Sylvia looks very attractive tonight. I've never seen her look lovelier."

Merry's heart sank. Surely not Benjamin, too!

"Better not let Stephanie see you making eyes at her, then," she said tartly, and Benjamin laughed with genuine amusement.

"Oh, I think I'm quite safe," he assured her. "Maybe I've got the experience behind me not to be so susceptible to feminine charms which resemble the froth on the cream. Perhaps I like a little more substance. As for Stephanie, she's got her own plans about what she wants."

"Well, perhaps you'll get the substance," said Merry, watching as Stephanie moved gracefully forward to a table in the centre of the room.

"I wondered if you'd all like to give an opinion on this enamelled jewellery," she was saying, unrolling a long velvet pad. "I've one or two pieces here, but I think their appeal will be a matter of taste. I should like to have your very honest opinion, though."

Eagerly the small party clustered round the table while Stephanie laid out a few lovely pieces. There was a brooch, shaped like a rose, in blue, a pansy with a checked design in green and black, a lovely bracelet of small interlocking squares in maroon and yellow, and one of oval-shaped pieces in green. The rich yellow gold, which formed the base, gave a glowing effect to the enamel.

"There are some cocktail rings, too," said Stephanie, laying out a large ring in very deep blue, with a strip of diamonds set in diagonally.

"I think they're fab!" cried Sylvia excitedly. "But if someone gave me a choice, I think I'd rather have something which looks real, if you know what I mean. These could look like Woolworth's."

"Oh, I don't agree," said Merry quickly. "There's something very special about all of them, a sort of richness and . . . finish, perhaps . . . which lifts them out of the ordinary. No, I like them."

"It's the design, I think," said Benjamin, picking up the rose brooch. "It's got beautiful balance and the workmanship is perfect. I like them, Stephanie."

"I wonder if they'll sell, though," said Nigel, frowning as he stared down at the table. "What's your opinion, David?"

The tall dark young man came forward to rest his hand on Stephanie's shoulder, then he sat down at the table and leaned his chin on his elbow, staring at the pieces intently. Quietly he drew an eyeglass from his pocket and examined each piece in turn.

"Beautifully made," he commented, "and I

expect Stephanie has chosen the best designs available, if I know her!"

He smiled up at the girl, and she flushed a little under his gaze. Merry had noticed before that David called the Kilpatricks by their christian names, though the rest of the staff referred to them as "Miss Stephanie" and "Mr. Nigel". That suggested quite a close relationship to her, though later she found out that David and Nigel had studied gemmology together, and David had been asked specially to run the Hillington shop. There was, nevertheless, a special relationship between them.

"We'll try a few, and give them good advertising. We have one or two very discriminating customers who might appreciate the unusual."

"Are you going to advertise them at your next cocktail party?" asked Sylvia.

"That's being held in the New Year," Stephanie told her, "so you might not be here for it. We don't want to disturb our stock until after Christmas and it does involve a lot of organising, and ensuring the safety of our stock."

"Oh, but I expect I will be here," said Sylvia sweetly. "Merry says I must consider Beau Ness as much my home as hers, and we're such good company for one another."

Merry felt her cheeks flush, and inwardly she tightened with anger against Sylvia for placing her in such an impossible position. She didn't really want Sylvia all that long, yet how could she fail to accept the situation in front of everyone?

Nigel, however, was looking delighted and making no secret of it, while Benjamin stood by quietly, an impassive look on his face.

"I am staying, aren't I, darling?" Sylvia was asking.

"If you want to," said Merry, and hoped her voice didn't sound as grudging as she felt. Sylvia seemed to have a disrupting influence on her life, but she could hardly throw her out, selfishly.

"Good, then I hope I can come to the party," said Sylvia, looking appealingly at Nigel.

"Of course you can," he told her, and Merry caught Stephanie looking at her sardonically. She smiled a little sadly, feeling suddenly out of things and a little tired. She didn't join in when Nigel began to make suggestions for having a small party at Christmas, and was glad when it was finally time to go home.

CHAPTER 6

A WEEK before Christmas, Aunt Elizabeth and Uncle George arrived to stay, and Merry welcomed them with mixed feelings. Christmas was a time for families to be together, but she'd never felt too much a part of their family.

"Will it be too much for you, Mrs. Cameron?" she asked anxiously. "I don't expect they'll stay long, because Uncle George still takes an active part in his investment business. He's only semi-retired, really."

"They'll maybe not find things as luxurious as they're used to, Miss Merry," said Mrs. Cameron, "but you know I'll do my best to make them comfortable. It's the first time I ever remember them stopping more than an hour or two. I don't think Miss Ellen ever found them bosom companions."

"They're all the family I've got," Merry said quietly.

"I know, Miss Merry. As a matter of fact, this house needs a wee bit of warmin' up noo and again. If they can take good plain service, then we might have a good Christmas."

"I'll help all I can," Merry assured her, and went to settle in her aunt and uncle. Sylvia had treated them casually at first, but was now eager to tell them all about Nigel and Rossie House.

"They've got fabulous jewellery, Mummy," she enthused. "In fact, I should just love one of their pieces for Christmas."

"No doubt," said her father dryly, "but for once, young lady, you'll have to set your sights a little lower. Neilson's is going through a bad patch at the moment. That's why I thought I'd like to come here for a quiet Christmas, and take up Merry's invitation."

In the end, it was one of the busiest Christmases Merry had ever known, as Mrs. Cameron took some time off to go and see her sister, and found both the Campbells feeling under the weather. Even the aspirin and cups of tea she made for them failed to make them feel better, and in the end they had to go to bed with 'flu.

Mrs. Cameron ran home to Beau Ness.

"Whatever will I do, Miss Merry?" she asked. "I just can't leave you with all this on your hands, yet they're both in bed. Fair bad, they are—helpless. Isa's temperature was a hundred and three and the doctor said I'll need to keep an eye on her. I really shouldna hae left them."

"Then you must go back, Mrs. Cameron," said Merry firmly. "We're all able-bodied here, and the others will just have to help."

"See that they do, Miss Merry. See that they do."

"I'll pop down to see you on Christmas Day," promised Merry. "There won't be so much to do since you've got nearly everything ready, and in any case, it won't be the first time I've cooked a Christmas dinner."

She bit her lip, remembering how she'd intended to ask Benjamin, then learned that he was already invited to Rossie House. She should have expected that, she thought unhappily, and maybe it was just as well if she was going to be in the kitchen most of the day.

Aunt Elizabeth heartily approved of Nigel when he called to take Sylvia out. At first he had also asked Merry, but last time she'd been much too busy, and now he made no pretence of wanting anyone else but Sylvia. Merry introduced him to her aunt and uncle while they waited for her to get ready, and they were charming to him.

"How nice they can be," thought Merry. "If only they were like this all the time, they could stay here always."

Yet some time, long ago, the Neilsons had reduced everything to the level of L.S.D. and made no effort to be charming when they didn't think it worth their while.

"I might find business a trifle boring because I don't understand it," Aunt Elizabeth was saying, "but jewellery is rather different. It's such an ancient craft, and one can so admire a beautiful piece of jewellery, because man has actually dug it out of the ground and applied his skill to making something of beauty which will last for ever."

"I suppose the same can be said for all forms of art, dear," Uncle George boomed. "Pictures, sculpture . . . that sort of thing . . ."

"Yes, but there's something very *personal* about jewellery," Aunt Elizabeth pointed out. "I mean you can't *wear* a picture. You can only admire it on the wall, but you *can* feel that a piece of jewellery is your very own. Isn't that so, Mr. Kilpatrick?"

Nigel was smiling, obviously charmed with both of them, then Sylvia ran lightly downstairs in the lovely new dress which Merry was struggling to pay for. She looked so beautiful that Nigel's face went pale at the sight of her, then he flushed vividly. Aunt Elizabeth and Uncle George were full of pride, but it was to Nigel that Merry turned, wishing she could say what was in her heart. She was still fond of him, and admired him, though she knew she wasn't in love with him.

"Be careful, Nigel," she wanted to say. "She looks so beautiful, and so grown-up, but underneath she's immature and irresponsible. Her heart still hasn't been touched . . . yet. She goes out with young men, and accepts their love because she enjoys it. It makes her love herself all the more. So please be careful!"

But Merry's thoughts and emotions had to be kept to herself as they waved the young couple away. There was still a great deal to do, and she would have to do it herself. Aunt Elizabeth had politely informed her of this.

"I've had to come here because George and I need a rest so," she told Merry. "Surely you don't think we'd enjoy burying ourselves in a backwater like Kilbraggan if we felt able to organise a normal Christmas, and dear Sylvia seems quite happy to be here at this time. It's all fitting in very well. The house is fairly comfortable, even if it is pitifully old-fashioned. Some of it is very shabby, Merry, and I'm sure you could do something with it without spoiling its character, if you like its old-world atmosphere. I mean, those velvet curtains are badly faded now. Why hang on to ancient things like that? New ones wouldn't be out of place. In fact, they'd make it a lot better. And that carpet in the hall is very worn ..."

Merry sighed. She'd already tried to explain to Aunt Elizabeth that there wasn't much money for extras, and she couldn't afford to replace a lot of furnishings, but her aunt had merely looked bored and said it was all a matter of planning.

So now Merry hurried back to the kitchen, and began to make rum butter. Uncle George liked everything that was traditional at Christmas. Ten minutes later, Aunt Elizabeth put her head round the door to tell her that "that young man" had called.

She'd already met Benjamin, but had lost interest in him from the start when she learned he was the artist living in the Cot House.

"Oh, dear," sighed Merry, looking round the kitchen. She had several things to do, then she must tidy it all up in case it got out of hand. Mrs. Cameron would be upset if her lovely kitchen became cluttered and soiled for her coming back.

"Benjamin can come in here," she said decidedly. "We're working together on a children's book," she added, as Aunt Elizabeth looked at her suspiciously and rather disapprovingly. She considered that Merry was inclined to be irresponsible in the friends she made. Some day she must explain all about Benjamin, thought Merry rather tiredly, but at the moment it didn't matter.

A moment later Benjamin walked through, a frown of displeasure on his face.

"What's the idea of this?" he said. "Cast yourself for the role of Cinderella? I saw Sylvia and Nigel go off gallivanting in his car, and I came over expecting that only desk work was keeping you at home. Now I find you're the scullery maid, waiting hand and foot on the aunt and uncle. Where's Mrs. Cameron?"

"Nursing her sister and brother-in-law. There's 'flu in the village."

"I know," said Nigel. "As a matter of fact, old Jake Grieve is down with it very bad. I hope he gets the spunk to fight it. I like that old boy."

"You know all the villagers well, don't you?" asked Merry softly.

"Yes, and I believe you're beginning to know most of them yourself. You've really settled down here, haven't you?"

"I love it," said Merry. "I wasn't awfully happy with. . . ."

She broke off, wondering why she was suddenly rambling on like this. It was none of Benjamin's business anyway.

"Then why land yourself with them like this?" he asked softly. "I don't mind seeing you work yourself to the bone in your own interests, or even for people you love and who care about you, but not after an ungrateful family. Your Aunt Ellen wouldn't like it."

"They're all the family I've got," she repeated to Benjamin, as she'd done to Mrs. Cameron.

"Well, you'd be better off without, as, I am," he said. "I don't like to see you slaving while others are enjoying themselves, and I hate a girl without spunk who just lets people walk over her, and take things away from her, while she doesn't lift a finger in protest. She just sits in the kitchen and lets it all happen."

Merry's cheeks flamed furiously. There were times when Benjamin went too far, and it angered her in spite of her love for him. He'd no right to talk to her like this!

"For heaven's sake, try to help yourself a bit more," he told her. "You know what you want, so don't let little butterflies like Sylvia steal your cake. Show a bit of fight, can't you?"

Merry's eyes cleared, as she realised Benjamin wasn't pleased about Sylvia going off with Nigel. He thought she still cared for Nigel.

"I don't mind Nigel taking her out," she said slowly.

"But you're still fond of him?" asked Benjamin.

Merry turned away, wishing she could explain that it wasn't love, because she now knew what love was. She couldn't bear the look on Benjamin's face if he found out she'd been stupid enough to fall in love with him. He might be kind, or he might try to laugh her out of it. Either way, she knew she couldn't bear it. Better to let him think it was still Nigel, so she just nodded a little.

"Oh well," he said, easing his bulk out of a sagging chair.

"There are all kinds of fools, and I can only think of one bigger one than you."

"Wait a minute, you haven't had anything to drink."

"And I don't want it," he returned, his face suddenly cold and hard. "Feed it to the relatives, then be sure you wash up and dry all by yourself, and put hot water bottles in all their beds, including Sylvia's. And you'd better sit up and wait for her, and have her hot drink ready, too."

Tears stung Merry's eyes.

"If you've said your piece . . ." she told him huskily, and Benjamin took her shoulders and turned her round to face him, then bent and kissed her swiftly.

"I suppose if you were any different, you

wouldn't be you," he said, roughly, "but I wish you'd start thinking of yourself for a change."

So that he wouldn't have to think about her, thought Merry dejectedly. The kiss had seared her lips and she felt her heart beating like an excited bird in her breast. Her tears spilled over as the door closed firmly behind him. Even if there was no Stephanie, he couldn't love her because he despised her and thought her soft and spineless. Sighing, she thought of the small secret gift she had bought him for Christmas in a moment of mad impulse. They were a small pair of lovely gold cufflinks, and as much as she could afford. Now she knew she must hide them away, and buy a tie or a book token. The gift would be a complete give-away.

Sylvia came downstairs the following morning with the news that she wanted to spend Christmas at Rossie House. She could stay there overnight, and have Christmas dinner with the Kilpatricks, who were having a small party.

"You were invited, too, darling," she told Merry sweetly, "but I knew you'd be busy here."

"But surely you'll want Christmas dinner with your parents, Sylvia," Merry protested. A day all by herself with Aunt Elizabeth and Uncle George wouldn't exactly be full of excitement.

Aunt Elizabeth wavered. It would be rather dull, with only Merry to keep them company, and if it hadn't been the fact that she hated cooking, it might have been better just to have her and George on their own. If only that Mrs. Cameron hadn't gone and taken 'flu herself now. Really, the place was most unhygienic, and she'd been having to use a gargle and mouth-wash herself, and encourage George to follow suit.

Still, she liked Sylvia being friends with the Kilpatricks. They were obviously people of substance, and Nigel was charming. Sylvia could do a lot worse for herself.

"All right, darling," she conceded. "I suppose it wouldn't be proper to hang on to such a popular girl as yourself at Christmas time. I expect we quieter ones will have to get along without you."

Merry bit her lip. She knew she ought to assert herself and refuse to be the doormat Ben-jamin accused her of being. She ought to insist that Sylvia should stay and help a little, then both could go to the party.

But she suddenly felt rather tired. She had to go to the village now, for some last-minute groceries, and to see Mrs. Cameron who had collapsed with 'flu after attending her sister. Merry had a nice gift for her, a neat brown handbag which she knew would match her coat, and she hoped it would cheer Mrs. Cameron up if she took it now.

There hadn't been much money for Christmas gifts, not after foolishly buying Benjamin that present, but she had tried to choose wisely. Now she wondered if her gifts weren't a bit dull, after watching Sylvia tie up several pieces of nonsense into fairy-like packages. Sylvia chose amusing, novelty things, or small pieces of luxury which rarely lasted after Christmas Day, but were lots of fun at the time. Nevertheless, it would have been nice to take her gifts to Rossie House and tie them to the huge Christmas tree to have them distributed by Mr. Kilpatrick in his Father Christmas costume. Instead, Merry found time to slip over to Rossie House on the afternoon of Christmas Eve and hand in her small parcels. The ones for Aunt Elizabeth and Uncle George she saved for Christmas day.

There was still magic about Christmas, thought Merry on Christmas morning. Aunt Elizabeth and Uncle George seemed to shed their veneer of selfishness and become quite sweet towards her. If only it would last! thought Merry.

By her plate she found several small packages which had been sent over from Rossie House, and the welcome gift of a good pair of gloves from Aunt Elizabeth and a bottle of perfume from Uncle George. Stephanie had chosen a book of poems, and Nigel's gift gave her a great deal of pleasure when she opened the long jeweller's box to find a pretty pendant. It was a tiger's eye, set in silver on a silver chain, and Merry loved it on sight. Later she found that Sylvia had also received a pendant, hers being a lovely cultured pearl in a gold heart-shaped setting on a fine gold chain. Sylvia admired it, but would secretly have liked something more flamboyant.

Merry set aside all packing, and her few small gifts including the wisp of lace handkerchief from Sylvia, and tried not to feel too disappointed that there was nothing from Benjamin.

Aunt Elizabeth and Uncle George complimented her on the Christmas dinner, then retired to doze a little and watch television while Merry cleared away. She was still polishing glasses, when the kitchen door opened, and Benjamin walked in.

"Why aren't you at Rossie House?" he demanded without preamble. "I seem to do nothing else these days but talk to you across a tea towel."

"Oh, Benjamin!" she cried, near to tears with sudden tiredness of spirit. "Please don't start again. Can't you wish me a Merry Christmas instead? Look what Nigel's given me!"

She held out the tiger's eye pendant for his inspection.

"Very nice," he said briefly. "Perhaps you'll find this a bit tame, then. Thanks for the tie, by the way."

She flushed.

"It was a poor sort of gift. Actually I . . . er . . . had something else in mind . . ."

She opened her small parcel, and exclaimed with pleasure at the dainty charm bracelet, with a tiny silver typewriter already fixed to it.

"I thought it might be fun to add a few charms now and again," he said awkwardly, and she felt a surge of pleasure at his words. Should she run upstairs and retrieve his cufflinks? she wondered. Then she bit her lip to restrain herself. Benjamin still belonged to Stephanie. Nothing had changed, nothing at all.

"Are you coming over now?" he asked.

"Has Stephanie . . . I mean, does she know you're here?"

"The Kilpatricks gave you a firm invitation for today," said Benjamin. "It was contained in a note sent to you via your cousin. I understand you only sent a verbal refusal, also via your cousin, and I was tempted to think you didn't get the note."

She shook her head.

"I didn't."

"Then get a move on. I'll wait for you. And don't keep throwing Stephanie at me every five minutes. Whatever you think of her, she's no fool."

"No," said Merry, "I know she isn't."

"I suppose Nigel ought to have come, but . . ."

"He's host, after all." put in Merry quickly. "All right, Benjamin, I'll change."

She put on a pale cream silk dress against which the tiger's eye glowed darkly brown, the pale line down the centre wavering constantly, then clipped on her charm bracelet. She brushed her russet-brown hair till it shone, and applied a bright coral lipstick, then stood back quite satisfied with her appearance. It was no good competing with either of the other two girls, and she didn't realise that there was a warmth about her which the other two lacked. She was soothing and refreshing, and deeply satisfying to look at.

Benjamin took her hand as she said goodbye to Aunt Elizabeth and Uncle George.

"But what about tea?" Aunt Elizabeth asked querulously. "Surely you are leaving no one in the house by going out like this? I've already explained that I'm in a very over-tired state at the moment, and any extra work is bad for me."

"There's plenty of turkey left, Aunt Elizabeth," Merry told her. "I've cut quite a few slices and there's salad already mixed, and Christmas cake."

"Well!" Aunt Elizabeth's tone wasn't at all mollified, and Merry found that Benjamin was gripping her arm tightly, his lips compressed. She knew he'd be furious if she changed her mind.

"I'm sure you'll manage," she said sweetly. "Don't wait up. I may be late."

"They're utterly selfish, and you don't

improve them one little bit," said Benjamin explosively, when they got outside. "You pander to them like a servant girl in Victorian times. You practically lick their boots!"

"It isn't true," protested Merry, laughing a little at his exaggeration. "Besides, they gave me a home when I had none, and I don't forget that."

"What sort of a home could those two give anybody?" he demanded. "Oh, come on before I start to shake you. And if you don't enjoy yourself this evening, relax a bit and have a good time, I shall push you in the loch at the next opportunity. You'll dance if I have to dance every dance with you myself."

"Don't bother," Merry told him. "I think I can find my own partners."

Rossie House was in a gay, festive mood, and Stephanie seemed genuinely pleased to see Merry, even if Sylvia's face momentarily took on a sulky expression, especially when Nigel came forward to greet her.

"The pendant's lovely," she told him, as he swept her into a dance. "It's so unusual."

"Rather like you, Merry," he told her seriously. "You look very pretty tonight."

"Thank you, Nigel," she smiled, her eyes suddenly bright. It was wonderful to feel gay and lighthearted again, and she looked round at the crowd of young people, many of whom she had met already. Stephanie was dancing with David

Bruce and Sylvia . . . Sylvia was dancing with Benjamin and smiling up into his face. Merry saw him smile in return and bend down to listen to something she had to say, then laugh with amusement. She looked away and smiled again at Nigel. She was fast getting to the stage where the very sight of Benjamin with anyone else was causing her pain.

"Why do I love him so much?" she asked herself. "Sometimes he isn't even nice to me, and hectors me shamefully, yet I only want him in the whole world. Why can't I accept that I can't have him, and learn to look on him objectively?"

But she could find no answer. She could feel the small charm bracelet, with the tiny typewriter, almost burning her flesh as she caught at it after the dance finished. Already it was very precious to her, and she caressed it gently. She must do as Benjamin suggested and have a gay happy time. Moping against fate never did anyone any good.

Nigel caught her hand and introduced her to several other young men, and Merry found, from then on, that she didn't lack partners, and was half pleased and half chagrined when Benjamin was pipped at the post once or twice. It would teach him to think of her as a Cinderella! When he finally did claim her they danced together silently, as though they were one person, and Benjamin thanked her gravely at the end.

Merry merely nodded in reply, wondering if he had felt the wild beating of her heart when he held her close. Vaguely she realised that she had expected that his engagement to Stephanie might be announced at this party, but nothing had been said, and she still wasn't wearing a ring ...

It was after midnight when Nigel took her and Sylvia home in the car. Sylvia was inclined to be sleepy and a trifle giggly. She'd been having cocktails, and had forgotten to count.

"It was lovely, Nigel darling," she crooned. "Lovely, lovely party! Lots of lovely things, too. Best party ever."

Nigel grinned as he escorted them into the house.

"I think you'll have to help this infant to bed, Merry," he said indulgently "She's enjoyed herself too much."

"I'll see to her," said Merry crisply, a sudden spark of anger in her eyes as she caught sight of the dining table. She was glad Benjamin wasn't here to see that Aunt Elizabeth and Uncle George had obviously made a good tea. The remains of it were still scattered all over the dining table and the room looked dirty and untidy with papers and magazines. It had been too much to hope that Aunt Elizabeth might clear away and wash up!

After Christmas, Merry again tried to concentrate on her work, though it was difficult with

Aunt Elizabeth and Uncle George still showing no signs of going home. They had begun to find the old house with its faded comfort very relaxing, and both spent long hours doing as little as possible while Merry tried to keep her home running. Mrs. Cameron was still at her sister's, getting over her bad dose of 'flu.

Sylvia was enjoying the festive season, accompanying the Kilpatricks and their friends to dances and parties, though Benjamin, too, had opted out as he had just received a batch of manuscripts to read, in order to do book jackets for them.

Two days before Hogmanay, Merry got up feeling headachy and rather shivery, so she dosed herself with aspirin and did her best to get through the day.

She prepared a light and not very appetising meal for Aunt Elizabeth, Uncle George and herself since Sylvia was lunching in Hillington, then sat down on the settee feeling her body aching strangely and her mind working feverishly and very clearly. Aunt Elizabeth was grumbling because the cheese had gone dry.

"I don't mind such a light meal, Merry," she was saying, "so long as it is nourishing, and I do think that a nice piece of steak or a chop is rather more nourishing than sliced Spam, even with potatoes and vegetables. One can always, of course, have a little more cheese and biscuits with the coffee, but the cheese was decidedly dry. Don't you agree, George?"

"Indeed I do, my dear."

"I consider that the fault lies with the local shops," she continued. "I'm not sure that the food they sell is fresh. I should insist on fresh food only, Merry, when you shop. Remember that, my dear."

Merry stared at her, seeing her a slightly grotesque caricature of herself, then very clearly indeed. Her cheeks flushed, and her flesh began to grow hot to the touch.

"I'm afraid you'll have to see to that yourself, Aunt Elizabeth," she said rather thickly, as she stood up unsteadily. "I shall have to go upstairs."

Elizabeth stared at her.

"Merry!" she exclaimed, outraged. "Surely you haven't been drinking the sherry left over from Christmas? Really, it's too irresponsible of you!"

Merry shook her head.

"No," she said, making for the door. "Sorry . . . I'm going to bed."

It was a relief to be in her own room, though the bed felt alternately cool and comfortable, then hot and unbearably lumpy. She felt as though she sometimes floated in the air, then she wanted to reach out for a cooling drink, which wasn't there.

As it grew dark, Merry suddenly blinked to find Aunt Elizabeth there, asking if she intended

129

to sleep all day. She shook her head, feeling perspiration stream behind her neck, then Elizabeth laid icy fingers on her forehead.

"How appalling!" she cried, almost accusingly. "You've got 'flu. You've been visiting that old woman, and have brought her germs here. I told you what would happen if you were careless!"

"Can I have a drink, please?" croaked Merry, and felt that the glass of water Aunt Elizabeth brought tasted like nectar.

Figures floated round Merry's head . . . Aunt Elizabeth, Uncle George and Sylvia looking a bit scared. Then Nigel was there, and Merry tried to smile at him as he bent over her, floated to the ceiling, then bent over her again.

"Nigel!" she cried weakly, then summoned a little more strength. "Nigel!"

He disintegrated into small floating objects, and changed into Benjamin.

"Her temperature is a hundred and four," he was saying. "Why couldn't you have rung Dr. Greer? And for heaven's sake, get Mrs. Cameron. She still isn't a hundred per cent, but she'd never forgive us for Merry being in this state without telling her."

Merry wanted to put out a hand and hold on to him till Mrs. Cameron came, but the knowledge that they were nearby rested and soothed her, and she slept.

It seemed a very long time later when she

woke again, to find Mrs. Cameron gently tidying her bedroom. The older woman looked a trifle pale, but her face was bright and she slipped lightly over to the bed when Merry called to her.

"I'm so glad you're here," she whispered. "Are you better?"

"Right as rain," Mrs. Cameron told her, then wiped her nose with a large white hankie. "Oh, Miss Merry, I should have been home before, leaving you like this to them!"

"Are they . . . are they downstairs?" Merry asked.

"No, gone, thank goodness, though Miss Sylvia is still here. Keeps telling us all that someone has to say and help, but if you ask me, she's only staying because it suits her." Mrs. Cameron straightened the bed, and bunched up Merry's pillow. "There I go," she said, in a more normal tone, "worrying you again, and you as weak as a baby after as good a dose of 'flu as I've seen. Mr. Benjamin has been a grand help. He's fair taken care of you."

Merry lay back, feeling at peace with the world, and contentment stole over her. No one else mattered at the moment, and all the small niggling things she usually worried about faded away. Benjamin had worried about her, and that meant . . . might mean . . . that he cared a bit for her.

"Mr. Nigel's been here, too," Mrs. Cameron

went on. "He's sent all these daffodils, all the way from Hillington."

"It's very kind of him," said Merry softly.

Two days later Dr. Greer allowed her to go downstairs, and Mrs. Cameron installed her on the settee, propped up with pillows and cushions. Sylvia was relieved when she realised Merry didn't particularly want her to hang around and keep her company. She was quite happy with a good book, though she was very pleased to see Nigel when he called in the afternoon.

"Well, young lady, you have given us all a fright," he told her, mockingly reproachful. "What do you mean by giving yourself such a dose of 'flu?"

"I didn't enjoy it a bit," Merry assured him laughingly, and he looked with concern at her small pale face and large, blue-shadowed eyes.

"Don't go overdoing anything, then," he said, seriously. "'Flu can be nasty. Besides, we want you better for the next jewellery display and cocktail party. It's at the Royal Hotel."

"Goodness, that's very grand," exclaimed Merry.

"You were so good at helping last time. I was hoping you'd be willing to do the checking again."

"But, Nigel dear, I said I could help if you like," put in Sylvia, rather plaintively.

Nigel laughed and tweaked a silver curl.

"You're much too pretty to do anything else

but enhance the scenery," he told her playfully, then coloured a little as he turned to Merry. "Not that you aren't just as beautiful, Merry," he said awkwardly, and she laughed with genuine amusement.

"No need to apologise, Nigel. We know what you mean, and of course I'd love to come and help with the checking if I can be of any use to you and Stephanie."

"She's sold on the enamel stuff now, she and David Bruce," he told her. "David predicts big sales for it, and Stephanie wants to model a few pieces."

"Can't I even wear something?" asked Sylvia with exasperation, and again Nigel laughed with amusement, though there was a light in his eyes as he looked at her. Merry watched him, and knew that Nigel was very attracted to her cousin, and might even have marriage in mind after he had considered carefully. Nigel, she now knew, never did really important things in too big a hurry. He was often impulsive, but only over small things.

"I have something in mind for you," he told her. "I thought the topaz . . . it's still to sell," he told Merry.

"I thought that was a lot less valuable," put in Sylvia, pouting a little.

"It is," Nigel told her, "but I think you'll agree that this particular topaz is . . . very pretty, isn't it, Merry?"

"It certainly is," she agreed, remembering the fabulous stone. It had made her shiver a little when she handled it, and she hadn't felt at all comfortable until Nigel locked it away. So far no one had felt able to afford it.

"By the way, I don't think I shall be able to go to that concert of pop music after all, Sylvia," said Nigel. "We're going to be very busy over the next two weeks, and I'll be working late most nights."

"But, Nigel darling, you promised!" she cried, her pretty brows wrinkled with disappointment.

"No, my dear, I didn't promise," he told her quietly. "I said I'd *try* to go."

"And I want to hear it," said Sylvia, a trifle sulkily. "Surely you can stretch a point for one night?"

Nigel's lips were firming, and Merry glanced away, caught by a movement at the window.

"It's Benjamin!" she said delightedly, and Sylvia rose gracefully and ran to let him in. Except for one very brief visit, Merry hadn't seen Benjamin since she was too ill to talk to him.

"Well, well," he said, standing for a moment to admire the cosy scene by the fire. "Quite a family party. Sure I won't be in the way?"

"Now that's enough of that, Mr. Benjamin," said Mrs. Cameron briskly, from behind him.

"I'm just making some nice tea for you all, and I've some of your favourite fruit cake. You were a good help when Miss Merry was so bad, so you aren't running away now."

"Yes, I wanted to thank you, Benjamin," began Merry softly.

"No need for that," he told her brusquely. "I did nothing clever anyway, except get the doctor. It's what anybody would have done."

Merry flushed a little at his offhand tone.

"Well, thank you, anyway," she said politely.

"I . . . er . . . I didn't bring flowers or anything because you seem to have plenty," said Benjamin, looking round at Nigel's massive gifts of spring flowers, before tucking into his tea. "I brought this instead, though."

He produced a folder, and extracted a letter which Merry took with a puzzled wrinkle on her brow. Then her face cleared, and she read it with delight.

"Why, Benjamin!" she cried. "It's an acceptance for our little book. That's marvellous!"

"Here's the cover," said Benjamin, producing a piece of card with a delightful fairy-like drawing of a pink caterpillar surrounded by the gayest of flowers behind which peeped several delightful little animals.

"It's lovely!" she cried, and Sylvia, too, exclaimed with delight.

"I never knew you were so clever," she told Benjamin, her lovely face suddenly alight with admiration. "It's gorgeous. Will it be in all the book shops, with your name on?"

"I hope so," laughed Benjamin, while Nigel examined the drawing, then handed it back with a nod of approval.

"I'm afraid I'll have to go now," he said, rising to his feet. "It's nice to see you downstairs again, Merry. I'll come again and see you as soon as I can."

"I'll show you out," said Sylvia, rising quickly and taking his arm.

Merry watched them go, wondering if Sylvia would take her opportunity and try to wheedle Nigel into a firm promise to take her to the concert. How immature and childish she is, thought Merry, with a sigh. Nigel and she might even be happy together, if only Sylvia would grow up.

"What's wrong?" asked Benjamin, hearing the sigh. "Things a bit complicated at times?"

"A bit," she admitted, with a rueful smile. "Though there certainly are compensations when you bring news of another acceptance."

"Does the . . . money suit you?" asked Benjamin, indicating the letter.

"Of course, but not fifty-fifty, please, Benjamin."

"Fifty-fifty or not at all," he told her curtly. "There would be no book if you hadn't written it."

She said no more. It would be most welcome,

she thought wryly, glancing at her desk where a pile of bills had grown. Christmas, with Aunt Elizabeth and Uncle George as guests, had been an expensive time for her.

"All right," she agreed meekily. "And . . . and thank you."

She lay back among her cushions rather tiredly, as Sylvia came dancing back, her pretty face alive and sparkling. No doubt she'd got her own way after all, thought Merry resentfully.

"Are you getting tired?" asked Benjamin bluntly. "If so, for goodness' sake, say so, and don't be so polite. I'm off!"

"Oh, are you going so soon?" cried Sylvia.

"It's time Merry had a rest," said Benjamin firmly. "Go and get Mrs. Cameron. As for you, Sylvia . . ." He paused, considering a little. "I could do with a bit of help over at the studio," he told her. "I need a blonde model. How about it? I'll pay you, of course."

"Benjamin!" she squealed. "Do you really mean it . . . have my picture on illustrations? Isn't that exciting, Merry?"

Merry felt too tired to do more than nod. She was beginning to feel slightly dizzy again, and was glad to see Sylvia being hurried out by Benjamin. It didn't occur to her that she might not feel so happy about that later.

CHAPTER 7

IT was almost a week before Merry felt well enough to get up for a normal day, and it took even longer before she could take up the threads of her writing again. The first draft of her book was almost finished, and she began to work on it again, slowly at first, then with enthusiasm which brought a surge of excitement. She knew she had put her best into it, and her main characters came through crystal clear as likeable people. But would it sell? she wondered. Would all this highly concentrated work be wasted? But even as she collected her work together, she knew that it hadn't been wasted. She was a better writer for having tackled a major piece of work, and even if her reward was just her own pleasure and satisfaction, it was enough.

Sylvia was still paying visits to the Cot House, and her conversation was now revolving quite a lot around Benjamin.

"He's really very attractive," she told Merry. "I wonder why I didn't notice before. He's almost as good-looking as Nigel, in a different sort of way, and he's awfully talented, isn't he, Merry?"

"Very," Merry agreed, with a small smile.

"I'm sure he'd make a fortune in London doing portraits. You should just see the one he's doing of me. He's got his illustration finished, but this is different. This is a real portrait, and

I have to sit like this, and put my hair over my shoulder like this."

Sylvia posed enchantingly, and Merry looked at her uneasily. Surely Benjamin, too, couldn't have fallen under her spell. Yet why not? She remembered them dancing together at the Christmas party, and his face as he smiled down at her. Very few men were able to resist Sylvia, and it took varying degrees of time before they realised her immaturity. She had imagined that Benjamin had already sensed this in Sylvia, and she began to wonder if that didn't matter any more. Enchantment rarely included common sense.

"Did you know he's the real owner of Rossie House?" Sylvia was asking, and Merry nodded.

"Well, I think it was mean of you to keep that to yourself," said Sylvia a trifle petulantly. "You never tell me anything. Mummy and Daddy didn't know, so they didn't really get to know Benjamin, did they? I mean, they might have liked him just as much as Nigel."

"I shouldn't have thought that ought to matter," said Merry dryly.

She glanced at the clock and decided that her small break after lunch had lasted long enough and it was high time she was back at her desk.

"Anyway, don't go making eyes at Benjamin," she said lightly. "He belongs to Stephanie."

Sylvia's eyes opened wide.

"Where have you been, darling?" she asked.

"It's ages since Stephanie thought of Benjamin. In fact, I suspect it was David Bruce all the time, only he was just the shop manager, and she wasn't sure about how her father felt. But it's O.K. really. He's awfully good family, you know, and Mr. Kilpatrick respects his judgement in business matters."

"How do you know all this?" asked Merry, her lips a trifle dry.

"She told me, of course. They're getting married in May, after they do up the flat above the shop in Hillington. Didn't you know?"

Merry felt stunned as she sat staring into the fire. What about Benjamin? Had he cared for Stephanie and she had let him down? Or was he . . . was he quite free to love someone else? Or . . . or was it Sylvia who was now holding his heart? Perhaps, being an artist, he could only really love beautiful women, and perhaps that was why he had now asked Sylvia to come and pose for him.

She caught sight of her own reflection in the sideboard mirror and sighed deeply. The 'flu had taken the sparkle and radiance she needed to bring any beauty she had to life. Now she looked just dull and rather plain, and she had a great desire to curl round in the settee and cry and cry.

"What's the matter? You look a bit strange," Sylvia told her.

"It's nothing. Just . . . I hope Benjamin hasn't been hurt by Stephanie, that's all."

"He didn't love her," Sylvia said sagely. "I knew that straight away. You can always tell when a man's in love, and Benjamin's in love all right, but not with Stephanie."

She stretched herself complacently, looking rather like a small golden cat.

"I've to go for another sitting tomorrow. Wouldn't it be lovely if he got an exhibition or something, the thing real artists get?"

"Benjamin's a real artist," said Merry shortly.

"Of course he is, darling. Haven't I just said so? I must go and ring Nigel, though . . . remind him about tonight."

Merry watched her glide away, and tried to adjust her ideas. But her head began to ache, and she lay back and closed her eyes, feeling the warm tears under her lashes. She felt rather than saw Mrs. Cameron bending over her, and tucking a tartan rug round her knees.

"It's the depression," she was saying. "It fair makes ye greet, but ye'll feel better after, Miss Merry. I grat mysel' to sleep one nicht, and a' for naethin' ".

Merry nodded, and began to enjoy her good cry. After all, it was just all for naethin'.

For the next few days, Merry couldn't settle to anything, though she began to type out the more straightforward parts of her book, then resolved to go and see Benjamin. His personality seemed to loom over her, governing her every action, and she was finding it more and more difficult to be completely independent when her need for him seemed to grow every day.

She chose a time when Sylvia wasn't with him, having gone to Hillington, no doubt to spend her fee on knicknacks, and used the straightforward excuse that she had come to see the portrait.

"I've heard so much about it from Sylvia," she said easily, "that I admit I'm curious, Benjamin. Can't I see it?"

He regarded her thoughtfully.

"Certainly, my dear. Come over here to the studio."

The portrait wasn't quite finished, but Merry gasped when she saw it. Sylvia's wonderful beauty seemed to leap at her out of the canvas, and she stared at it, feeling her heart squeeze with pain. Benjamin must really have fallen in love with her, or he could never have painted her looking so unbelievably lovely.

"Is that how she looks . . . to you?" she whispered.

"That's how she looks to most people, I would imagine," Benjamin told her dryly. "Is it a good likeness?"

She nodded, biting her lip.

"No wonder she was pleased," she told him, keeping her voice light.

Benjamin covered the portrait up again.

"It's nice to see you more like your old self," he told her, "though you've still got to find your bit of sparkle. What about relaxation? Still going out with Nigel?"

She nodded. "He's asked me to help again with the jewellery cocktail party. I know you don't like me doing it, but I helped Stephanie last time because they were short-staffed, and now I know how to go about it. I'm helping to check again, and I shall enjoy it, really I will."

"Well, I suppose I can't influence you against it, though I still think they have no right to ask you," he said firmly.

He was looking much more serious and thoughtful than she had ever seen him, and it struck her that he was looking rather pale and thin. There was an unhappy twist to his smile now, and Merry had to control herself to keep from slipping her arms round him to comfort him.

"Is . . . is everything all right?" she asked softly.

"I wish it were," he said with a sigh. "I only wish it were, but I'm bad at trying to arrange other people's lives, my dear, especially when it touches my own. Do . . . do you think Nigel Kilpatrick still . . . admires Sylvia?"

Merry's cheeks coloured.

"I don't really know," she said, in a low voice.

"Can't you make sure he doesn't?" he asked,

an exasperated note in his voice, "if you care at all for him, that is."

There was a long silence while Benjamin stared out of the window, and Merry felt as though her heart was swelling to bursting point inside her. Benjamin was actually appealing to her to take Nigel from Sylvia. He wanted Sylvia, only Nigel stood in the way, and he wanted her ... *her* ... to try to gain Nigel's attentions!

Anger began to claw at her, anger fanned by jealousy, and she jumped to her feet.

"You aren't very good at arranging people's affairs, as you say, Benjamin," she said icily. "Why can't you leave me alone?"

"And why must you always be so spineless?" he demanded. "It's Sylvia take all, isn't it?"

"It seems to be," she agreed. "No doubt that's the way you want it."

Benjamin's face whitened.

"No doubt it is," he said tiredly. "I've done my best, Merry. I can't do more."

She didn't know how to reply, so she snatched her thick mohair scarf, and tied it round her head.

" 'Bye, Benjamin. It's ... it's a lovely picture."

"Perhaps I'll give it to Kilpatrick," he told her bitterly.

CHAPTER 8

MERRY bought a new dress for the exhibition, a beautiful gold sheath which made her russet-brown hair sparkle with copper lights. Sylvia sulked a little when she saw it, and grumbled at the small allowance she had been receiving from her father.

"I think Daddy's growing very mean," she pouted. "He says his income has been reduced, but he's always grumbling about money, though he manages very well. I wish I could have another dress. I don't suppose . . .?"

"No," said Merry, very firmly. "That new one you bought on my account will be quite good enough, Sylvia, and I'm not staking you to any more clothes. Why don't you get a job, anyway, and earn yourself some pocket money?"

Sylvia flounced round the room.

"What sort of work could I do?" she demanded. "I'd hate having to get up to go to an office or shop every morning. It would be absolutely ghastly, and Mummy wouldn't approve at all."

Merry thought of the two articles and story which she had just had rejected. Unless a miracle happened, and she sold her book, then she might need to find a job herself.

"Other people have to," she said slowly.

"I could always be a model, I suppose," said Sylvia, stretching her arms behind her head, "like I did for Benjamin. That wasn't too bad. Though maybe I'd be better to think of marriage. Maybe it's about time I settled down, though it's been fun having lots of boyfriends . . ."

"Anyone in mind?" asked Merry, rather too quickly, and Sylvia grinned at her wickedly.

"Perhaps," she said impishly. "Wouldn't you like to know? Which one would you like me to leave for you, darling? That just might . . . I say, *might* influence my choice."

Merry's face was scarlet with annoyance. Sylvia was outrageous at times, and took no thought of anyone's feeling but her own.

"Why should you imagine that I'd enjoy accepting what you leave?" she asked icily. "Anyway, I've always believed that people marry for love, not for any other reason. I would have thought that would govern your choice. It would certainly be the only reason for me."

Sylvia looked at her sideways from under her long lashes, and filed her immaculate nails.

"Want me to guess who it is?" she asked, swinging her long legs on to the settee. "You should learn to cover up your feeling a bit better. It saves embarrassment for the poor chap when he sees poor females wilting for love of him."

"Be quiet!" snapped Merry, her face now deathly pale. "You go too far, Sylvia. My private life is my own affair, and no one else's."

Sylvia's eyes widened at Merry's anger, and she tried to shrug it off with a slight smile.

"Goodness, darling, you do get worked up! I was only teasing."

"All right," muttered Merry, and went off to find Mrs. Cameron, her inner peace in a turmoil. How *could* Sylvia say such things to her? Yet was it true that Benjamin had noticed her growing love for him? Was that why he obviously wanted her to be special friends with Nigel? Her head ached again, and she began to wish she had never come to Beau Ness. She had been almost happier as an upper-class servant to her aunt and uncle. At least, that was how she had always felt. She had never been a daughter in their house, though Sylvia looked as though she was now considering herself part owner of Beau Ness without taking any part of the responsibilites.

"Benjamin's right," thought Merry dispiritedly, "I am spineless. I should ask Sylvia to leave, and concentrate on my writing."

She could love that enough to make herself a happy life, with only Mrs. Cameron to keep her company. The prospect felt very attractive at the moment.

Before the exhibition, Merry went over to Rossie House and helped Nigel by typing out a list of goods to be shown. She was quick to see how to prepare the list, as each item was ticketed, one side with red ink denoting the stock number, and the other side with the price, in code.

"I don't know how we managed before you came, Merry," Nigel told her, as she took a neatly tabulated list out of her typewriter. "Any time you need a job, there's one waiting for you at Kilpatricks."

Merry paused to look at him thoughtfully.

"Is there?" she asked.

"You know Miss Lennox left to get married," he explained. "We haven't been able to find a suitable replacement yet . . . one who is wholly competent and trustworthy. Mistakes can often mean quite a loss, you see. That's why I've been so grateful for your help, and hope you won't be offended if we offer you a small fee."

Merry saw that Nigel was being very straightforward and businesslike, and regarded him, consideringly.

"Thank you," she said, quietly, "and Nigel . . . if my book is hopeless, perhaps we could talk about that job again. Is it a deal?"

"It's a deal," he agreed, and bent to kiss her lightly.

"Oh, am I interrupting? Sorry!"

Colour flew to Merry's cheeks, as Benjamin stood regarding them from the doorway.

"I'm looking for your father, Nigel," he said. "I need his help over a form I have to fill in."

"He's in the room across the hall with Stephanie and David," said Nigel, though there was a frown of annoyance on his face. He hated being caught at a disadvantage.

"Thanks," said Benjamin, and smiled briefly as he closed the door.

"Sorry about that," said Nigel, glancing at Merry.

"Oh, I don't suppose Benjamin would mind," she told him, in a low voice. "We'd better do the animal brooches now. Isn't this little gold hedgehog with ruby eyes sweet? And this tiny bird with its nest of pearls for eggs? I do think they're dainty."

"I like this dog with the diamond collar," Nigel told her, his good humour quickly restored, "and the cat with the moveable head and tail." He laid out the beautifully designed animals in eighteen-carat gold, all encrusted with jewels.

"I expect Sylvia would like this one, though," he went on, smiling indulgently as he picked up a small poodle completely encrusted with diamonds.

Merry nodded, but made no remark. There was tension in her home now, and it was beginning to get on her nerves. Soon . . . very soon . . . she was going to have to ask Sylvia to leave.

The Royal Hotel had the finest reputation in Hillington and Merry liked its atmosphere of quiet good taste and slightly faded decor. The room which had been set aside from Kilpatrick's jewellery exhibition was in dusty pink and gold, and this time Merry felt no stranger to the proceedings as she pinned her small white button to her dress, and watched Sylvia delightedly doing the same. The colour had been changed for security reasons.

Nigel had brought them both, but now he left the girls outside the ladies' cloakroom, and went to check up on several things and see about displaying the stock on the usual stands. Stephanie was supervising the models, and David Bruce was in charge of the stands. Once again Merry was helping with checking the lists of special pieces being worn by the models, though she herself would not model any pieces this time. Sylvia, however, was delighted when Nigel asked her to wear the pink topaz ring. She had fallen in love with it at first sight, and was very thrilled at being allowed to wear it.

As they went to the changing room to join the other girls, they found Stephanie busy with instructions, though she turned to smile a welcome at Merry and Sylvia. She now wore, very proudly, a surprisingly small engagement ring on her left hand, and when Sylvia, with her usual thoughtless candour, remarked on this, Stephanie only smiled serenely.

"David insisted on affording the ring himself," she said, a hint of pride in the toss of her head. "It's my own choice."

Merry found this new Stephanie much more likeable, though Sylvia considered she had grown rather dull.

"She's just the type to end up a *hausfrau*," she remarked to Merry later. "That type always does, once she's kicked over the traces."

"She looked happy," defended Merry, "and I'm glad. She's not exactly a bosom friend, but she's straightforward and I like that."

Now Stephanie was giving each girl a number, and writing it down against the sets of jewellery they were going to wear.

"When the girls return," she told Merry, "you can check each item, see that it's put in its velvet case, and Nigel will pack the boxes into the fitted case. Got that?"

"Just like last time," smiled Merry, though she was interested to see the new selections. She liked the pearl and turquoise set, which consisted of a multi-strand necklace of cultured pearls with a turquoise-studded gold fastener. This had a matching bracelet and brooch. There was also a set in rubies and diamonds, with sapphire and diamonds in a similar design.

One of the models, clad in a sheath of purple velvet, was wearing a heavy gold necklace and bracelet. Merry looked at the number on her list and saw that it was described as a collar necklace.

"It's very heavy to wear," the model confided to her, "but somehow one doesn't mind. It looks so magnificent."

"Do you like doing jewellery?" Merry asked her.

"Yes, I think I like it best, though I enjoy the furs, too."

A firm of furriers, whom Nigel knew well, were exhibiting their furs first of all, and Merry went with Stephanie and Sylvia to sit at a small side table, and watch this with interest. The guests were all present by invitation, and again Merry found them an unusual mixture. Some obviously admired the beauty of the finished product, while others considered it in terms of cost. Merry liked to look at the overall attractiveness of each outfit, and especially liked the small fur hats which matched the coats.

Soon, however, it was their turn, and the guests were milling round the stands, admiring the lovely pieces of jewellery which were being displayed, and relaxing again for the final mannequin display.

Merry enjoyed it all hugely, though part of her felt her responsibility keenly as she checked off necklaces and ear-rings, putting them into velvet-lined leather cases, while Nigel packed them into a square fitted case.

Sylvia was in her element, as she walked down the floor, a vision of pale silvery beauty, and displayed the huge and very beautiful pink topaz ring while Mr. Kilpatrick commented on it, giving the size in carats, describing the setting and quoting its price. Sylvia's eyes were brilliant with excitement when she finally took the ring back to Merry.

"It's absolutely wonderful," she said, popping it into its case. "It's the most fabulous ring ever. Have you marked it off, Merry?"

She nodded, bending over the paper, ticked the number, then passed on the ring box to Nigel. There was only the diamonds which Stephanie was wearing. They, too, were what she had worn before, with the addition of a trembler brooch. This was shaped like a spray of flowers, each flower head being set on a small spring, so that the brooch shimmered and trembled under the bright lights.

"I hope some of our old dowagers buy them this time," said Stephanie, as she took off the pieces and packed them away. "I think the ring might go, though. I saw a few drooling faces ... though it's a bit pricey."

"I like the pearls best of all, though they're a bit pricey, too," said Merry.

"You must find yourself a rich husband," said Stephanie without the old sardonic note in her voice.

"Yes, I must," smiled Merry.

Her smile felt a little stiff, though. She had looked in vain for Benjamin that evening, and learned later that he'd had to go to London, unexpectedly, on business.

Perhaps that was why the evening went flat on Merry after a while, and she was glad when the last of the pieces had been put in the cases, and the strong fitted jewellery case and leather briefcases had been locked away.

Nigel took them all back to Rossie House for coffee and the very welcome sandwiches, and Merry discovered that she was hungry. She didn't care for champagne, and there had only been a few crisps and nuts by way of eats. Now she ate the dainty chicken sandwiches with enjoyment and was able to join in the general excitement. Sylvia seemed to glow like a jewel herself, though, and Merry looked suspiciously, once or twice, at her flushed cheeks and shining eyes. Surely Sylvia hadn't been drinking more than one glass of champagne!

Nigel, too, was staring at Sylvia, rather like a moth fluttering round the flame, and Merry wondered how long it would be before his heart took charge of his head, and he asked Sylvia to marry him. Her attraction for him was now obvious for all to see, and she saw Stephanie's small frown of annoyance, and wondered if her cousin would really be welcomed by the Kilpatricks. That Nigel would be welcomed by Aunt Elizabeth and Uncle George was a foregone conclusion.

Merry sighed and wondered a little about

having Sylvia living permanently close to her at Rossie House. Was she unnatural because she couldn't love Sylvia as much as she ought to love her only cousin? Marriage might improve and settle her, thought Merry hopefully, and got to her feet deciding that it was time to go.

The following Monday morning, after breakfast, Nigel telephoned and asked if Merry and Sylvia could come over to Rossie House. It was urgent.

"You go, darling," yawned Sylvia. "I feel tired today, and it must be for something dull when it's just after breakfast. I mean . . . an invitation to do something exciting would come after lunch or in the evening, wouldn't it?"

"Nigel said both of us, and it's urgent," said Merry firmly. "He sounded . . . upset . . . or something. Or he could have been excited. Perhaps he's sold the ring!"

Sylvia examined her nails, then jumped up and fussed over some magazines. She had been a bit restless over the weekend, and Merry suspected that she had been waiting for Nigel to call her on Sunday, and had been disappointed. Now she didn't want to appear too eager to see him.

Or could it mean that she was missing Benjamin, too? Merry had felt strangely lonely, knowing that the Cot House was empty, as though a light, however flickering, had suddenly been extinguished. Nothing seemed right with her world, now that Benjamin wasn't standing by.

"Come on, Sylvia," she said, a trifle impatiently. "The Kilpatricks want to see us. I don't think we can completely ignore their invitation, do you?"

"Oh, all right," agreed Sylvia, "I'll come this time," and watched Merry quickly sort through the early morning post. "By the way, have you heard if you've sold your book yet? Will . . . will you get a lot of money?"

"I've only an acknowledgement," Merry told her. "I'll just have to wait until I do hear, though it's very important to me. I'm afraid to think how important. I don't think it will earn me much money, but even a little would help. The little children's book I did with Benjamin is going to bring in a little, but not nearly enough. I may decide to take Nigel up on the offer of a job. Maybe that's why he wants to see us . . . offer us a job, I mean."

"Not me, darling," said Sylvia, shaking her head, as she buttoned on her warm woollen coat. "He wouldn't offer me a job! That's not what interests me at all. How are we going to Rossie House? Is he sending the car?"

"Ten minutes' walk," said Merry firmly. "Don't be mad, Sylvia. Come on. I'll just tell Mrs. Cameron in case we're late back for lunch."

There was an air of disturbance about Rossie

House when they arrived and a rather scared-looking Jeanie Lumsden took their coats and showed them into the study where they could hear several voices talking angrily and excitedly.

"Ah, here they are," said Nigel, as they walked in the door, and Merry looked swiftly round the group, seeing Mr. Kilpatrick standing by his desk, his face pale and drawn. Stephanie, too, was pale and haughty-looking, while David Bruce's face was red with anger.

Merry could feel Nigel's fingers trembling on her arm, as he led them into the room, and soon everyone was shouting again, while questions reeled about her head.

"Wait a minute, wait a minute," cried Nigel. "One at a time! Merry! Do you remember checking the topaz ring?"

Merry looked bewildered.

"Of course I do."

"And you got it back from Sylvia?"

"Of course she did!" cried Sylvia indignantly.

"Of course I did," nodded Merry. "I marked it off."

"What did you do with it then?"

"Gave it to you, Nigel. It was in that small blue leather ring case."

"Well, it's not there now!" cried Stephanie. "What do you have to say to that?"

Merry found that she couldn't say anything. Sylvia was staring, wide-eyed, at the empty box, her face suddenly pale with fright.

"I . . . I can't understand it," said Merry.

"Think, my dear," said Mr. Kilpatrick kindly. "Was anyone near you at the time?"

She shook her head.

"Any of the staff . . . any of the models, even?" broke in David Bruce. "It's always the staff who get blamed, you know!"

"Nobody's blaming you, and you know it," cried Stephanie. "If I blame anyone, it's Nigel for influencing us into allowing outsiders to help. What do we really know about . . . ?"

"That's enough, Stephanie," said Mr. Kilpatrick sternly. "You know we had Miss Saunders well checked out before she came here, and the report was excellent. Her family is beyond question."

Merry's face had gone very pale. So these people had actually had her investigated? Sudden distaste for everything to do with Kilpatricks filled her, and she wanted to leave the house right away, and never come back. Benjamin had been so right. She should never have taken anything to do with checking their stock, only she had been too stupid to see where the danger lay. If only he had been here, his very presence would have been a source of strength to her, but now there was only Sylvia, and even she felt suddenly dear to her, part of something familiar instead of this strange frightening world into which she was peeping.

"Sylvia, my dear, you came off the floor

wearing the ring?" Nigel was asking quietly, and she nodded, her eyes enormous.

"Yes," she croaked.

"Now think carefully. You see, dear, this is such an unusual ring. We couldn't ever replace it, because a stone of that large size and purity doesn't turn up every day."

"But wasn't it insured?" asked Sylvia, a sudden air of shrewdness in her manner. "Surely, if it's lost, you can get the value of it."

"Only if we can prove there was absolutely no negligence," said Nigel quietly, "and somehow we've slipped up here. Someone, unnoticed, has been around . . . some thief . . . ready to seize their chance. Only one of us must have noticed, even if we've forgotten, and somehow we must bring it to mind. We'll have to inform the police, but I've persuaded the others to wait a day, in case we can fathom out where it has gone. We only want the publicity of the police as a last resort."

"The police?" whispered Sylvia, and Merry, too, felt her face go pale at the thought of being involved in the disappearance of the ring. She *did* check it. She remembered Sylvia handing it to her and the feel of the blue ring case in her hand. She had given it to Nigel after marking it off.

"I don't think anyone else was there," she said slowly.

"We don't *want* to suspect . . . anyone," said Stephanie gruffly. "But we might be forced to, if it doesn't turn up."

"But there's only . . . us," said Merry slowly, and her remark trailed into uneasy silence. Surely they couldn't suspect . . . her? She felt panic rising inside her, and had to force herself to sit quietly, and see things from the Kilpatricks' point of view. They had lost a unique and valuable ring, and could be forgiven for starting to look around at suspects. And it was she who had been checking! Oh, why hadn't she listened to Benjamin?

"We shouldn't have given Merry the responsibility," said Nigel heavily. "Stephanie is right, in part. We shouldn't have asked Merry to take on such a job."

Again the remark fell into silence, and Merry thought, rather bitterly, that she'd have preferred to hear him proclaim her innocence, instead of reproaching himself for giving her the responsibility.

"Go over every minute again," said David Bruce almost desperately. "Sylvia, you are walking off the floor."

She nodded.

"What did you do then?"

"I . . . I was wearing the ring on my left hand," she said huskily. "I took it off with my right. The blue case was on the table, and I put it in. I told Merry how much I . . . I loved and admired it, then I gave it to her, and she marked it off."

"That right, Merry?"

She nodded, feeling as though her body suddenly didn't belong to her. That was right. That was how it had happened. And she gave it to Nigel, who put it into the fitted case, and locked the lid. Nigel was the only one with the keys . . . but Nigel wouldn't steal his own ring.

That left her . . . left her . . . She lifted her hand to her head, feeling as though the walls were screaming at her.

"I don't *know* how it can be missing," she cried wildly. "You must know I didn't steal it. I admired it . . . we all did . . . but I'd be mad if I'd tried to steal it, because . . . because . . . I couldn't *do* such a thing. I'd hate it always . . . afterwards. Don't you see?"

"Of course you wouldn't take it, darling," Sylvia said soothingly. "It must just . . . have . . . gone missing somehow?"

"Where did the case go after you left the Royal, Nigel?" asked Merry.

"It's no good," said Nigel heavily. "It went straight into our safe and Father and I have half the combination each. No one touched it till we opened it this morning and found the blue ring box empty."

He looked at Merry's face which was almost transparent with the upset.

"I'd better take the girls home," he said

heavily. "If . . . if you can think of anything, anything at all, come and see me. We call the police in at noon tomorrow."

Merry nodded, and almost ran out into the fresh air, breathing deeply. All three drove home to Beau Ness in silence, where they found the parcel post van standing at the door, and Mrs. Cameron signing for a parcel.

"It's for you, Miss Merry," she said, handing it over, as Merry and Sylvia walked in the door. Merry nodded, this time feeling the tears well up in her eyes. It was easy to recognise the returned manuscript of her book.

The rest of the day was the longest Merry had ever known. Sylvia had been very restless, too, and after prowling up and down the house for a while, and going to annoy Mrs. Cameron in the kitchen, she flung herself on to the settee.

"I think I'll go home, Merry," she said sulkily. "Everything seems to be getting in a mess here, and I'm fed up. Nigel hardly bothered with me today and Benjie is away, and I'd like to see the gang again."

For a moment Merry felt a treacherous lightening of spirit as she began to imagine the house without Sylvia, then remembered that her peace was shattered in any case now. Besides, with the loss of the topaz ring hanging over their heads, and the police due to be informed, it was hardly a wise time for Sylvia to leave.

"I doubt if you can, Sylvia," she said wearily. "I mean, if Nigel tells the police, they'll be bound to want to question you . . ."

"I haven't done anything!" screeched Sylvia. "Why should they bother with me?"

"You've handled the ring, of course," said Merry evenly. "They have to question everyone connected with the exhibition in a case like this."

"But I gave it to you!" cried Sylvia. "You know I did!"

"I know," Merry replied patiently. "You'll still have to tell the police that."

Sylvia sulkily picked at her nails.

"I wish I'd never gone to the wretched exhibition," she said, almost passionately. "Mummy will be livid if she hears about the police. So will Daddy. He might even . . ."

"Even what . . . blame me?"

"I was going to say that he might even cut off my whole allowance," snapped Sylvia, and Merry wondered by how much she had got into debt before seeking refuge in Beau Ness. Merry knew that her home had only been used as a refuge by her cousin, until Nigel started taking an interest in her. Would he still be interested in Sylvia, she wondered, or would all this upset make any difference?

Besides, what *could* have happened to the

ring? Could there be two small blue leather boxes? Was it possible the ring was in another one? Merry's eyes grew round with thought, then clouded again as she remembered that the whole of the black fitted case had been taken out and examined. If there had been two such boxes, Nigel would know, and would have examined the other one.

Yet it was unthinkable that any of them could be a thief, Merry was sure of that. Somehow . . . somehow that ring had gone missing accidentally, if she could only think when, how and where.

Mrs. Cameron was ill pleased at their small appetites for tea. Merry had told her, briefly, about the ring, and she shook her head uncomprehendingly.

"You shouldn't be worrying your heid ower it, Miss Merry," she pronounced. "Eating like a wee sparrow won't bring a ring back. It'll turn up, never you fear. From what you say, it would be a daft-like thing to steal it, for everybody would ken it in any case, and the thief could neither wear nor sell it."

"That's right," agreed Merry, brightening. "It must turn up somehow, Mrs. Cameron. If only it could be soon!"

Both girls went to bed early, but Merry lay tossing and turning, her mind too busy for sleep. She went over the events of the previous evening till her head ached, but had no recollection of anyone else being close by them.

Finally she got up and padded to the bathroom for aspirins, seeing a light under Sylvia's door as she returned to her own room.

"Poor Sylvia," she thought with sudden sympathy. It had upset her cousin, too, and perhaps even more so, if she was beginning to care for Nigel. She heard small sounds of drawers being pulled open, and paused on her foot. Surely Sylvia wouldn't be mad enough to be packing so that she could sneak away. It would be just like her to do that!

Resolutely Merry went to her cousin's door, and tapped firmly.

"Sylvia," she said, opening the door, then stopped with bewilderment at the state of the room. Sylvia was, indeed, packing for a quick removal. As Merry opened the door, she whirled round guiltily with a quick surge of breath, her hand to her mouth.

Merry stared at the hand unbelievingly, at the pink topaz ring which was winking back at her.

"Sylvia!" she whispered. "For heaven's sake! You've got it!"

Her cousin tore off the ring and threw it on the dressing table, then dropped on to the bed, her face white as a sheet.

"What if I have?" she cried defiantly.

"But why . . . how . . . ?" Merry's brain

seemed to be alternately racing and clouding.

"Easy," said her cousin. "I had it in the box to let you see, then slipped it out again while you bent to mark it off. It was in the palm of my hand, till I could pop it into my bag."

"You must be mad!" cried Merry. "Stark staring mad!"

Sylvia began to sob.

"Well, it's *my* ring," she cried childishly, "and no one would buy it for me. It's no use asking Daddy, and when Nigel talked about us getting engaged, he thought I was joking. He . . . he even said he . . . he thought we ought to think a bit longer about marriage, that I was obviously too young! He was backing out, Merry, and from a girl who could have married anybody."

Merry watched her with fascination, then all the fight and spirit seemed to drain out of her.

"I was mad," Sylvia said quietly. "I know it now . . . completely mad. I couldn't resist it. It was as though the ring was part of me, and I couldn't give it up. Oh, Merry, what shall I do?"

"Take it back," she said firmly. "Own up and make a clean breast of it. They won't tell the police, I'm sure, so long as you give it back first thing in the morning."

Sylvia was silent, then she turned huge tragic eyes to Merry.

"How can I?" she asked brokenly. "There's

something you don't know. I'm in love with Nigel . . . really in love. I knew it today for the first time when I realised I'd lost him. Oh, Merry, there might have been a chance for me, and I'd do my best to make him happy. Honestly. I feel . . . different . . . now, as though I've grown up all of a sudden. I feel ashamed of the girl I was. Merry, couldn't you take it back? Say you've found it caught on your dress or something? They couldn't prove anything against you, and it won't matter to you since you don't love Nigel . . ."

"I couldn't!" cried Merry, horrified. "They'd never believe me. They'd think I'd stolen it."

"They wouldn't," insisted Sylvia. "They know you too well. Oh, Merry, if I can't have a second chance, I think I'll die."

Sylvia broke into a storm of weeping which shook her whole body, and Merry stood hesitating, the ring in her hand, her body shivering again as it did when she handled the topaz. For her, all its beauty had gone, and she only wanted it out of her home. She had always felt odd about it, and now she knew why. She looked at Sylvia tiredly, no longer feeling able to cope.

"All right," she agreed, "but on one condition. You must leave my house. If Nigel wants you, he can follow you home to Carlisle. I don't think you can remain here, with this between us, and I'd rather that Aunt Elizabeth and Uncle George were responsible for you."

"All right," agreed Sylvia. "I was going anyway. I'm tired of it all."

Next morning Merry walked over to Rossie House, feeling as though she was wading through the ocean. Her face was deathly pale and set when she was shown into the study where Mr. Kilpatrick was working on his own.

"Here is the ring, Mr. Kilpatrick," said Merry, without preamble, and tried to tell him she had found it by accident, only the words stuck in her throat.

"I . . . I can't explain how I found it," she said quietly, and watched him pick it up for examination.

"Yes, it's our ring," he said at length. "But I think I'm entitled to the fullest explanation . . . where it was found, how it came to be missing. Come . . . ah, Merry, perhaps you would be good enough to explain. Otherwise," he added, as she stood tongue-tied, "Otherwise I shall be forced to put the worst possible conclusions on the circumstances."

"Will . . . will you inform the police?" she asked, with apprehension. If so, she might be forced to tell them about Sylvia, and if she did, would they believe her now?

He regarded her searchingly, his eyes beginning to glint.

"No, I shan't inform them, but only because you've been a guest in my house and come from a fine family. I know your Aunt Ellen, and your father . . . well, I'm sorry we won't be able to entertain you again. This house is full of temptation to young ladies who can't resist the lure and sparkle of precious stones. I blame myself for not realising how strong such temptation can be."

Merry wanted to cry at the sudden softening and kindliness of his voice. Her knees were trembling and she felt strangely sick.

"You may go home now," he said gently. "If you don't wish to meet my son and daughter, you'd better go now. It might be embarrassing for all of you."

Merry nodded and stumbled from the room. She almost ran home, feeling again the emptiness of the Cot House as she raced past. If only Benjamin had been home. He'd never have believed her a thief, she was sure. She wanted him and needed him, but he wasn't there. Then she remembered that she had no claim at all on his time, and felt more lonely than she had ever done in her life as she walked into Beau Ness.

"That Miss Sylvia is away, bag and baggage," Mrs. Cameron told her angrily, as she walked into the kitchen. "Trust her to hang on here, then run away at the sight of unpleasantness! She's a selfish young madam!"

Merry nodded wearily.

"I knew she was going, Mrs. Cameron, but I

forgot to tell you. You'll be glad to know the ring has been found now."

Mrs. Cameron's face relaxed into a beaming smile.

"Och, didn't I say so all along?" she asked, delightedly. "Was it just mislaid?"

"Something like that," Merry told her evasively.

"A big fuss about naethin'! Och, Miss Merry, you're no looking like yoursel' today. If you ask me, you've never quite got over that 'flu. Though maybe I can guess what's wrong."

Merry held her breath.

"It's yer wee book," continued Mrs. Cameron. "Och, ye're bound to be disappointed, but don't let it get you down. Miss Ellen often had setbacks, but she took them in her stride. Ye'll have to start another book as soon as you can, and learn from past mistakes. Now come on and take this hot drink. I'll be able to feed you up now that fussy madam is away."

Merry felt comforted. Mrs. Cameron often talked good horse sense.

CHAPTER 9

THE following morning Merry got up, heavy-eyed through lack of sleep. The house felt calm and peaceful without Sylvia and Mrs. Cameron was singing softly in the kitchen, but Merry felt tired and depressed. The full realisation of the fact that the Kilpatricks thought her a thief was beginning to dawn on her, and her whole being cried out in protest. She felt unclean, and wanted to run all the way to Rossie House and deny the fact that they thought her guilty of stealing. Yet she would have to tell the truth about Sylvia, and would they believe her? Even if they did, Sylvia was still a member of her family, and it would make little difference to her future relationship with them. There could still be nothing between her and the Kilpatricks.

Wearily she picked up her returned book manuscript, and began to undo the paper. Perhaps the publishers had given a reason for its return, and it would be helpful to know where her fault lay.

The letter was a long one, giving quite a lot of praise, but pointing out quite a bit of her plot construction which was faulty, and suggesting alterations.

"If those passages could be altered in the way we suggest," the letter concluded, "we would be happy to consider the book again."

Merry read and re-read the last paragraph, her heart beating excitedly and her depression lifting miraculously, then carefully she read the whole letter again, referring repeatedly to her manuscript. Of course, she could see now where she had gone wrong, and how much better the book would be with the suggested alterations.

Energy and enthusiasm pulsed through her, and she ran to find Mrs. Cameron.

"Yer breakfast's just ready now, Miss Merry," said Mrs. Cameron, fussing over her like a mother hen.

"Oh, not very much this morning," Merry told her hurriedly. "I've got heaps of work to do, and I want to get it done quickly."

"Ye'll do it all the better on a good full stomach," the older woman said firmly. "After that, I'll see ye're not disturbed. It's fine to see a bit of life in ye again, if I might say so."

Merry ate up her breakfast, her mind already busy with the book.

The next three days passed in a dreamlike state of hard work and snatched meals against Mrs. Cameron's approval. Merry was aware of her hovering in the background, an air of uneasiness about her, but she put everything but her book out of her mind, and soon it was again ready for posting and Merry lay back in her easy chair, feeling drained but at peace. Whether it was now accepted or not, she felt she had done a good worthwhile job, and her body and mind were soothed with satisfaction.

She jumped up and put on her warm anorak and gloves. She would feel even better when the book was once again in the post.

"Anything from the village?" she asked

Mrs. Cameron, peeping into the kitchen.

The woman looked up at her, pale-faced, her eyes clouded.

"Er . . . no, Miss Merry . . . that is, I'll be getting it a' masel' when I see what's needed. Er . . ."

"What?" asked Merry.

"Naethin'," mumbled Mrs. Cameron unhappily.

But Merry was in the third shop before her suspicions were confirmed that some people were looking askance at her, as though wary and suspicious, while others were over-hearty as though anxious to show that they were on her side.

She walked home, feeling the nightmare begin to close round her again. Surely the whole village didn't suspect her of being a thief? It was pretty obvious that the story of the missing ring had leaked out, and where it had come from. Jeanie Lumsden, the cook at Rossie House, was a great gossip, and knew practically everyone in the village.

Merry thought of Mrs. Cameron's unhappy looks, and anger began to rise in her. Surely her own housekeeper hadn't been listening to tales against her . . . and believing them! She remembered that Mrs. Cameron and Jeanie Lumsden were cousins, and the knowledge did nothing to cheer her up.

When she got home she walked straight to

the kitchen, where Mrs. Cameron was peeling potatoes.

"Well?" she asked bluntly.

"Oh, Miss Merry!" The older woman's eyes filled with tears. "I've been that mad at Jeanie Lumsden, and we're not talking noo. But she swears it's true about . . . about that ring. She says they suspect you of keeping it deliberately, though ye took it back rather than get the polis. I've tellt them till I'm tired ye couldna hae done sich a thing. It's far more like that Sylvia, but they say it was you handled the ring. I feel that ashamed anybody could suspect you, and a cousin o' mine could spread the word, though many a one is sidin' wi' me and sayin' ye couldna hae done sich a thing. There's been a mistake somewhere."

Merry looked her straight in the eye.

"You honestly believe that, Mrs. Cameron?"

"I do," said the other woman simply. "There's two ladies I've served an' I'd lay my life doon against their honesty and good name. Miss Ellen and you, Miss Merry. But . . . but I feel that frustrated. Could ye no get these rumours stopped, Miss Merry? Make that Kilpatrick crowd apologise in public, or something? There was jist something aboot them I never trusted. Mind you I suppose they think it's a' still private, an' forget Jeanie Lumsden is slippin' roon the hoose when they talk aboot private things. She's no sense of loyalty, an' that's why this is the first place she's kept, an' that only because servants are scarce nooadays. Could ye no demand an apology?"

Merry sat down and closed her eyes. She couldn't let herself be suspected like this! She just couldn't! Yet what could she do about it now? See Nigel? Would he believe her? She would have to tell him all about Sylvia. Would he suspect it was only a fit of jealousy?

"I thought people would have . . . would have known me better, Mrs. Cameron," she said, a trifle huskily. "I . . . I thought I had some friends down in the village."

"And so ye have," said Mrs. Cameron staunchly. "I'd like to crack some of their heads together. They've little else to think about except scandal, where they can find it."

Sudden distaste for everything filled Merry's heart, and she looked round the room she had come to love. Even this beloved house felt alien to her, set amidst pointing fingers and accusing stares, and she felt she could no longer bear it. Ever since she had walked back from Rossie House, after handing back the ring, she felt in her heart that she must leave this place, and start afresh elsewhere—Edinburgh, perhaps, or even London where few people would even have heard of Kilbraggan. She would go into Hillington straight after lunch, and see an estate agent.

The following day a well-dressed middle-aged man arrived in a large comfortable car and was conducted over the house, making notes on a pad.

"It won't be too easy to sell, Miss Saunders," he warned her. "It's a charming house, but not everyone wants old property these days. They like new, streamlined kitchens, and rooms easy to keep clean. Still, I'll put my board up, and advertise in all the best papers and magazines. We'll view by appointment only, and that will make it easier for you."

"Very well, Mr. Grant," said Merry quietly. "I'll leave that to you."

She watched him go, while Mrs. Cameron walked up and down the house, pale and silent, her mouth drawn with disapproval.

"You're sure to be all right," Merry told her comfortingly. "I'm sure that whoever buys the house will need someone to help, so you'll be able to stay on."

The older woman looked at her levelly.

"If you weren't upset, ye couldna say sich a thing tae me, Miss Merry," she said flatly. "Dae ye think that's a' I care aboot . . . my job? No, I hate to see ye running away, as though ye're admitting to everybody that the rumours are true. That's what I hate."

"I don't think I care any more what people think," said Merry wearily. "I've tried to be happy here, to work quietly, and mix in with the community, and somehow I've made a mess of it. I'm tired of it all, Mrs. Cameron."

176

"Dear knows what Miss Ellen would have to say if she knew," said Mrs. Cameron darkly. "She'd sort them out before I could flick my feather duster!"

"Oh, Mrs. Cameron!" wailed Merry, and burst into tears.

The housekeeper sat down beside her, and drew her into comforting arms.

"There, there, ye're just a bit bairn," she said compassionately, "and even if the new folk go down on their knees to me, I wouldna stop here and leave you on your own . . . wherever you decide to go. Ye need somebody to look after you, an' that's a fact." She stroked the soft brown hair. "It's time Mr. Benjamin was home," she said firmly. "He's another one who can sort them. He'll not listen to a load of nonsense, won't Mr. Benjamin."

Merry only cried more than ever.

CHAPTER 10

LATE on Sunday evening Benjamin returned home again, and on Monday morning he made his way to Beau Ness.

Merry saw him from the window, and had an almost overpowering impulse to rush out and throw herself into his arms. She controlled herself, however. She had been rejected by enough people over the past few days, and if Benjamin didn't want her, or even if he pretended to want her out of pity, it would be the last straw.

Mrs. Cameron let him in, and he came striding straight through to the study and stood, white-faced, glaring at Merry. She saw that he was in a towering rage, and she stiffened inwardly, her chin firming as she met his eyes squarely.

"I want to know all about it," he told her quietly. "All. Every word. Tell it . . . from the day I left for London."

"There isn't much to tell," said Merry, her voice croaking with nerves.

"Not much? My God! Now, just you start talking, and tell me it all. We'll start from that damned jewellery exhibition."

Merry wet her lips and nodded, pausing a little to assemble her thoughts. Her writer's mind gathered it all together coherently, and quietly she began to tell Benjamin about the exhibition, the checking, the missing ring, and the fact that she found it that evening in her own home.

"How did you come to find it, and who had it?" demanded Benjamin.

"I have nothing more to say," she told him stubbornly. "The Kilpatricks have their ring back again. They didn't call in the police. As far as I'm concerned, the incident is over."

She looked at him and caught her breath. His face was deathly white, and his eyes blazed with furious anger.

"You have nothing to say," he said, in a very quiet, controlled voice. "You helped the Kilpatricks. They lost their ring . . . you recovered it. Now they . . . they think you're a thief. You . . . you accept that. You even put Beau Ness up for sale! And you've nothing to say!"

The last words seemed to vibrate round the room.

"Sylvia has gone, like a rat deserting the ship," continued Benjamin, prowling round like a caged bear. "Have Nigel Kilpatrick or Stephanie been in touch with you?"

She shook her head, and Benjamin stopped prowling and stood straight in front of her.

"I've never heard anything so . . . so . . . shameful in all my life," he told her, in the same quiet, controlled voice. "I . . . feel like giving you the spanking of your life . . . and as for Kilpatrick . . . !" Words seemed to fail him. "Don't move from here, or do anything, till you hear from me again," he told her, as he made for the door. "Is that understood?"

Merry wanted to ask why he should dictate to her, but she felt too miserable to speak, and could only nod dumbly. She was too numb even to cry. Benjamin found her . . . shameful. She sat very still, not wanting even to catch sight of herself in the mirror. Reluctantly she answered the telephone, to find that it was Mr. Grant, the estate agent. He said he wanted to see her, and made an appoinment.

Later, at tea-time, Mrs. Cameron tried to tempt her with some tender roast chicken.

"Mr. Benjamin hasn't stayed long anyway," she remarked, and Merry shook her head, thinking of the brief, stormy interview. "No, our Isa saw him pelting off for the station again after a visit up to Rossie House. She says he was in a bad mood, too, for he never even looked at Cailleach, and he always has time for that wee dog. Got real fond of him after you saved him from the tinkers."

That seemed centuries ago, thought Merry sadly. Those days seemed like another world.

"I haven't seen her for a week or two myself," said Merry. "She's such a dear wee dog."

"Then why don't you pop over to see Isa this afternoon?" pleaded Mrs. Campbell. "I've got some things to send ower to her, and ye could do wi' a wee walk. Isa would fair welcome you. She's nearly eaten anybody who had a word to say against you, and that's a fact."

Merry considered, then lifted her chin. Why not? Her conscience was clear, and she could look anyone straight in the face.

"Why not?" she asked. "I'd like that, Mrs. Cameron."

"That's a good girl," beamed the older woman.

It did Merry good to have a rapturous welcome from Cailleach, when she arrived at the Campbells' cottage, and for Isa, too, to welcome her with open arms.

"Come away in, Miss Merry. I've been fair wearyin' to see you again," she said. "Our Bessie gives me all the news, but it's not the same as seeing you. I've been baking, too, so we'll just get the kettle on and have a wee cup of tea."

"That will be lovely, Mrs. Campbell," sighed Merry, while Cailleach tried to make up her mind whether to settle on her knee or lick her ears and chin.

"She's full of energy today," said Merry, trying to settle the little dog.

"Och, she's been fine ever since her fright," said Isa, "as though she can never be grateful enough to be back home. She's easily frightened by anything strange."

Merry nodded. She knew how the little dog felt. Soon she too would be changing her way of life, going into something strange, and in spite of all that had happened she knew that her heart was still in Kilbraggan.

As though in answer to her thoughts, Isa Campbell turned quickly to look at her.

"We'll be right sorry if you go away, Miss Merry," she said, with customary directness. "I could have cried when our Bessie told me. And all thanks to our own kith and kin, too . . . Jeanie Lumsden. She got a warming up from me, I can tell you!"

"The circumstances weren't Jeanie's making," said Merry quickly. "It was . . . it was . . . just an accident."

"Well, all right-thinking folk in Kilbraggan will not stand by and see you insulted, Miss Merry. That we'll not! You'll see."

"Thank you, Mrs. Campbell," said Merry humbly. "It's done me good to come and visit you."

"Have another bit of cake, then," coaxed Isa delightedly, and Merry did.

She walked home from the Campbell's feeling much cheered, till she passed the Cot House again. Where was Benjamin now? Anyway, it didn't matter. He hadn't even told her he was sure she was innocent of theft. He'd only been angry at her story.

The following evening Mrs. Cameron showed an unexpected visitor into the sitting-room, where Merry was quietly reading.

"Nigel!" she cried, leaping to her feet.

"Hello, Merry," he grinned sheepishly. "Sorry I haven't had time to come before."

Her chin lifted a little.

"Please sit down, Nigel," she said politely. "Would you care for some sherry?"

"That would be very nice," he told her, and

she poured a glass with hands which trembled slightly.

"I don't know how to begin to apologise," Nigel went on awkwardly. "Father wants to come and see you, too. He's very sorry he . . . he ever accused you . . ." He broke off with embarrassment.

"It was understandable," said Merry, feeling slightly bewildered. "I gave him the ring back without . . . without explanation."

Nigel nodded and bit his lip.

"Why didn't you say it was Sylvia?" he asked, a rough note in his voice.

Merry eyed him searchingly, feeling a pang of sympathy when she saw the look of sadness in his eyes. She was still bewildered. How did Nigel know it had been Sylvia?

"How did you know?" she whispered.

"She . . . she telephoned, and owned up," he said heavily. "I'm going to see her tomorrow. I . . . I was beginning to care deeply for her, but this has confused things. She behaves like a child at times."

"She must be growing up, when she has owned up like this," said Merry gently. "I must say I hadn't expected her to do that."

Nigel stared moodily into the fire, and shook his head.

"She only did so because Benjamin Brendan made her," he said quietly. "He came to see us in a towering rage on Monday, and asked if none of us had any brains or wits enough to see that you couldn't be dishonest if you tried, and were obviously covering up for Sylvia."

"Benjamin did this?" cried Merry, her heart beginning to thud with excitement. Benjamin had cleared her name . . . Benjamin!

"He raged at us all, then said if we wanted it from the horse's mouth, we could have it, and took the train from Carlisle. This morning Sylvia telephoned and spoke to Father, then to me."

Nigel was silent for a long moment, and Merry watched him, not daring to breathe.

"She sounded . . . different," he said, "and said if we wanted to . . . to prosecute or anything, she would take her medicine. She . . . she said she hadn't any excuse to offer."

"It was just a silly, stupid impulse," said Merry, but she knew that it meant a great deal more than that to Nigel.

"Be kind to her," she begged impulsively, as she went with him to the door to show him out, and he looked down on her small, vivid face and smiled gently.

"You're a dear and wonderful girl, Merry, and I'm a fool," he said softly. "Sometimes one sees the right path when it's too late."

She tilted her head inquiringly, but he only smiled again, obviously not intending to offer an explanation.

"Goodnight, my dear. Are we forgiven?" he asked.

"Of course you are," Merry told him, and he bent and kissed her swiftly before swinging off down the drive. She watched him go, and looked at her watch, debating. Was Benjamin home now? Was it too late for her to go and see him when every instinct wanted to take her to the Cot House, to thank him for believing in her?

She came back in and shut the door gently. It was too late, but time now seemed to stretch before her into eternity. She now felt so close to Benjamin that she could reach out and touch him beside her. They had all their lives ahead of them, and she could wait patiently for tomorrow. Mr. Grant was coming in the morning, shortly after breakfast, but she would see Benjamin after lunch . . . unless he came to see her first!

The morning brought no sign of Benjamin, though Merry hummed happily as she put on a well-fitting tweed skirt and soft cashmere sweater before Mr. Grant came at ten.

The tall, grey-haired estate agent looked very pleased with himself when Mrs. Cameron showed him into the sitting-room, and Merry rose to meet him with a smile. She'd been having second thoughts about selling the house, now that her innocence had been proved, and she no longer felt an atmosphere of suspicion around her. Yet the whole affair had been distasteful to her, and she felt as though Rossie House seemed to tower over her. Besides, she was very much aware of Benjamin close by, at the Cot House, and felt that she wanted to see him before making up her mind.

She explained all this to Mr. Grant, as gently as she could.

"Please don't think I'm shilly-shallying," she pleaded. "It's just that . . . well, things have been rather upset recently, and I'd like to feel more settled before I finally make up my mind to sell Beau Ness."

Mr. Grant pursed his lips.

"I'm very sorry about that, Miss Saunders," he told her. "Very sorry indeed. As I said before, houses like this one just aren't easy to sell, and it's very gratifying to be given a substantial offer for it, very gratifying indeed. I don't know if our client would be willing to wait a long time while you make up your mind. I doubt if you're likely to get such a fine offer from anyone else."

Merry also bit her lip, wishing she could think a little more clearly.

"I wonder how long he would give me," she said tentatively.

"I could let you know, of course," Mr. Grant told her. "I could see him before I leave Kilbraggan. He lives in the village here."

"Lives here?" echoed Merry, a frown between

her eyes. Who, in the village, could afford to make such a good offer for her house?

"May I know who has made this offer?" she asked, her voice suddenly cool and practical.

Mr. Grant hemmed and hawed for a moment.

"Well, I haven't been asked to keep the buyer's name private," he said at length, "so I don't suppose it will do any harm to tell you. It is Mr. Benjamin Brendan."

Benjamin! Benjamin wanted her house! That meant he must want to get rid of her!

"Thank you, Mr. Grant," whispered Merry dully. "I . . . I'll have to let you know . . . about . . . about selling to Mr. Brendan."

"Think over what I've said, Miss Saunders," Mr. Grant told her briskly. "It's an excellent offer. Good morning. Write or telephone when you've made up your mind."

"Good morning," said Merry chokily, feeling her legs trembling beneath her. "Please don't bother to see Mr. Brendan till you hear from me."

She wouldn't just move out and let Benjamin live here. It would be bad enough to go away and leave Beau Ness behind her, but to leave them both together. That would be too much.

She would have to go and see Benjamin, and know exactly how things stood. She would go after lunch.

Merry looked in her wardrobe after lunch,

tempted by a sudden desire to dress up and give herself confidence, but in the end she decided to be sensible and wear her green slacks and anorak. It was a cold day, and she must wear warm clothing, and besides, it was no good trying to impress Benjamin!

He stared at her unsmilingly, when he opened the door.

"Hello, Merry, doing me the honour of a visit? Come in and get a warm by the fire."

She followed him silently, removing her cap and gloves, then flopped down on to the settee, watching him clean a spot of paint off his hands.

"Mr. Grant's been to see me," she told him flatly. "Benjamin, why do you want Beau Ness?"

He frowned as he laid down his paint rag, then came to sit opposite her.

"Why are you selling it?" he countered.

"I haven't made up my mind that I am . . . yet," she said slowly. "After all that unpleasantness . . . with the ring . . . I felt I wanted to get away. But now . . ."

"Now everything's all right again," said Benjamin, in a hard voice. "Now everyone knows the truth, and Nigel's forgiven you."

She looked at him, wondering at his harsh tone.

"I should have thought you'd be pleased," she said, puzzled. "After all, I've you to thank for putting everything right again."

"Yes, I did, didn't I?" he laughed. "Didn't I? I made it all nice and cosy . . . for Kilpatrick to move in again. For heaven's sake, Merry, how much do you want me to take?"

She looked at him with bewilderment.

"I . . . I don't understand."

"Don't you? You must be very dim, my dear. Where's your pride, when you can keep running to that . . . that *bore* at the drop of a hat, as soon as he lifts his little finger? He can let you be thought a thief, and do nothing to protect you. He can go off philandering with the fair Sylvia, and come cheerfully back again when he finds her wanting . . . and you still welcome him with open arms. His conduct is shameful . . . yes, shameful! And so is yours, for meekly taking it all, and for wanting a man who treats you this way instead of realising that you're worth more than all his damn diamonds put together. 'Who can find a virtuous woman, for her price is far above rubies'."

"But I don't want him!" cried Merry, when Benjamin paused for breath.

"Don't lie to me, Merry," he said harshly.

"I *don't* lie," she retorted, outraged. "It's you who are jumping to conclusions . . ."

"I said don't lie," he repeated, gripping her arm. "I walked over to see you last night, after I got home from Carlisle, and I saw Kilpatrick leaving. I . . . I saw you kiss him . . ."

He threw away her arm roughly, and she

massaged it lightly where it still tingled from the pressure of his fingers.

"You saw me saying goodbye to him," she said tonelessly. "He doesn't love me. It's Sylvia he wants, though he realises there are difficulties. I doubt very much if he'll marry her."

"And you just sit and pine!"

"Why should I?" she asked tiredly. "When I don't care what Nigel does. I don't love him. I thought I did once, but I found I didn't when I fell in love with . . ." She stopped and bit her lip. ". . . someone else," she ended.

There was a long silence, then Benjamin spoke to her urgently.

"Who, Merry?"

"It doesn't matter," she told him quietly. "You wouldn't really be interested. I'll go now, Benjamin. You can have Beau Ness, if you really want it."

As she stood up, he rose, towering over her, and grabbed her by the shoulders.

"Who, Merry?" he demanded very quietly.

"All right, since you really want to know. It's you, Benjamin. Now you really know the sort of fool I am!"

But the last words were spoken against his shoulder as he just held her and held her, while the clock ticked gently on the mantelpiece.

"Have I been a fool?" he asked at length. "Eaten up with jealousy of Nigel Kilpatrick?

You . . . you said you cared for him when I asked you."

"I did like him," she said, her eyes clear and honest, "but I never really loved him. It was always you, Benjamin, only there was Stephanie."

"Stephanie?" he cried.

"I thought you loved her, you see. She seemed to want you."

"To tell her troubles to," said Benjamin, with a laugh. "Surely you must have known she wasn't my kind of person?"

"How could I?" she asked. "You even seemed to want Sylvia at one time."

"Sylvia? You thought I wanted Sylvia? I only tried to keep her away from Kilpatrick, just to give you a clear field if you wanted him, even if I thought he wasn't quarter good enough for you. Merry darling, are you sure you love me? I . . . I can't get used to the idea."

She nodded, her eyes shining, and he kissed her gently, then with deep purpose.

"We can be married soon, can't we?" he asked quietly. "Oh, and I shall want to buy Beau Ness. That is, if you still want to live there, darling."

"Of course I do," she said softly. "I'd live anywhere with you. Why *did* you want it?" she asked curiously.

"Because I couldn't bear to think of anyone living in your house. That business I had in

London was partly visits to my lawyer. I had some money coming to me, and that's all been settled now. I've also got some new contracts for my work, so we should be quite comfortable, darling. In fact, the lease of Rossie House is up in about two years. If you like, we could think of going back there, though it's never really been home to me. We might have our children to think about, though."

Merry smiled, her eyes shining at the future which lay ahead. She began to feel Aunt Ellen's presence very close to her . . . Aunt Ellen who also might have been mistress of Rossie House. Soon she hoped to hear about her book, and because it was Aunt Ellen's story as much as hers, she hoped she would sell it.

"Penny for them," said Benjamin, tweaking the end of her nose.

"I was just thinking how happy I am," she sighed. "Yet last week . . ."

"Forget about last week," said Benjamin, "and always remember that to me you are far above rubies."